Then Came Violence

Other mysteries by John Ball in Perennial Library:

Then Came Violence

John Ball

PERENNIAL LIBRARY

Harper & Row, Publishers, New York
Cambridge, Philadelphia, San Francisco, Washington
London, Mexico City, São Paulo, Singapore, Sydney

All of the persons depicted as lawbreakers in this book are fictitious.
Many of the members of the Pasadena Police Department are not.

A hardcover edition of this book was originally published for the
Crime Club by Doubleday & Company, Inc., in 1980.

First PERENNIAL LIBRARY edition published 1988.

Library of Congress Cataloging-in-Publication Data

Ball, John Dudley, 1911–
  Then came violence.

  1. Title.
[PS3552.A455T46 1988]   813'.54   87-45595
ISBN 0-06-080833-7 (pbk.)

88 89 90 91 92 OPM 10 9 8 7 6 5 4 3 2 1

For Dr. Shogo Takayama
and his lovely Nobuko
with warm friendship

1

It was only a little after ten o'clock when the two young blacks, both wearing jackets, came into the small grocery and liquor store. There was nothing unusual about them, particularly in that neighborhood, but when the man at the check-out stand saw them, he froze in his tracks. They were strangers to him, but just the way they had walked in told him at once that it was going to be another holdup.

He fought down his rapidly rising panic. He had already been robbed twice at gunpoint and both times he had been in great fear for his life. He had been extraordinarily lucky and had escaped without a scratch, but he couldn't expect that kind of reprieve again. He moved slightly to the right, where he could press the robbery alarm with his foot the moment he was sure.

Less than five seconds later the black closest to him whipped out a gun and yelled, "Freeze!"

The clerk rocked back and raised his hands, using the motion to cover the hard pressure with his foot. Then he held perfectly still, not giving the bandit with the gun the least excuse to shoot. But he had seen the man's face and didn't give himself more than a 5 per cent chance to escape unharmed.

The call went out from the Pasadena Communications Center at exactly 10:17 P.M.: "Fair Oaks and Hammond: a two eleven silent. Twenty-four Boy five, code three."

The dispatcher knew that would trigger some heavy action: in addition to the unit designated to respond with lights and siren, plenty of backup would also roll. Every patrol and supervisory car within a five- or six-minute ETA would be burning rubber within seconds, headed toward the location with roof lights on. The helicopter on ground alert three miles from the scene would be airborne in about ninety seconds.

The alarm had come from the predominantly black area. The watch commander, who was black himself, knew that heavy trouble could be coming down fast. White holdup men were usually content to take their loot and flee; blacks, the crime reports showed, were much more likely to murder their victims—especially if they were white, and the night clerk at the store in question definitely was.

The man at the cash register remained perfectly still, his hands raised. The second black was controlling the few customers in the store, a powerful .45 in his hand. His arm twitched as if he were anxious to shoot.

The first bandit shoved his gun directly into the clerk's face. "Give me the money!" he ordered.

The clerk obeyed immediately, glad that he no longer had to look the man in the face. He depressed a register key and when the drawer opened he began to hand over the contents. He did it fast enough to satisfy the holdup man while still taking as much time as he dared to give the police a better chance. There was another hidden alarm there, but he knew better than to attempt to touch it. If the store had been cased, which was almost certain, the man who was confronting him would probably know that. And there was no need: He had already tripped one alarm and the Pasadena Police did not need to be told twice.

As he continued to hand over the money, his life was in the balance and he knew it. He saw the young black with the gun steal a glance at the location of the hidden alarm; the fact that he had not tried to touch it could mean the difference between life and death.

And the fact that there were four or five customers in the store also increased the odds in his favor. If he had been alone and had been the only one able to identify the

2

bandits, his chances would have been nil.

When he had handed over the bills, the clerk began to pass over handfuls of change. He continued to move at the same speed; fast enough to get by, slow enough to give the police the maximum edge. He was down to the nickels when he detected the first sound of a siren.

"Now the back room," the bandit ordered. Then he heard the siren too.

"Cops!" he yelled to his partner. He whipped his arm back and smashed the barrel of his gun across the clerk's face. The man's legs gave way under the massive shock and he slumped to the floor, barely conscious, but in blazing pain. Dully he thought that if that was all he would have to take, he might yet escape with his life.

The two blacks sprinted out of the store, skirted around it, and then dashed into the anonymous darkness of the nearest backyard. Running like maddened eels, they worked their way to the end of the block, where they had left a car parked in the deep shadows of a driveway. Seconds later they drove slowly out and turned up the street, one driving and the other holding the paper sack with the money.

In one more minute they were out of the immediate area. The driver began to relax his shoulders a little. "That shithead," he said. "He hit the alarm. I'm gonna go back and kill him!"

His companion said nothing; he was still watching out for cops. When one of the white Pasadena patrol cars went past, he felt a sharp spasm in his stomach, but the police unit didn't U-turn and fall in behind them.

When the driver had crossed over the Foothill Freeway, he began to feel reasonably safe. All the witnesses would be able to tell the pigs was that two blacks dressed in dark clothing had scared the hell out of them. The three honkys would never be able to give a facial description and the other blacks wouldn't—he was sure of that.

He took the Pasadena Freeway into Los Angeles, knowing that as soon as he reached the south central area it would be all their way. They had money now, and the honky that had hit the alarm was going to suffer for weeks for trying to do in a brother.

The first unit to respond pulled up with a screech. Two patrol officers jumped out; while one of them crouched behind the engine hood, covering the front doorway, his partner, shotgun in hand, raced for the back. A second unit was right behind; the two patrolmen in it swiftly took up positions on each side of the doorway. Then, covered by the officer who was shielded by his car, they went in, ready for instant action.

Within five seconds they knew that the bandits had fled. A swift interrogation of the customer nearest the doorway yielded a minimal description of the suspects. As other units began to saturate the area, one of the officers inside took his portable radio from his Sam Browne belt and put the information on the air. According to the witness, the suspects were last seen running around behind the store less than two minutes ago.

The field sergeant arrived and took command. Overhead the bright light from the helicopter moved from backyard to backyard, illuminating the area and making the ground search vastly easier. A paramedic unit pulled up and the two men in it ran inside with their equipment. While other patrol units set up an outer perimeter, looking for a vehicle (no description) containing two male Negroes, eighteen to twenty-five years old and wearing dark clothing, the paramedics carefully loaded the injured clerk onto a gurney and sped away with him toward Huntington Memorial Hospital.

The field sergeant put out a code four, advising that no more help was needed at the scene. By the time ten minutes had passed since the first alarm, it was evident that the two bandits had made their escape, at least temporarily.

The sergeant called the witnesses together, apologized for detaining them, and delegated four of the officers on the scene to begin taking statements. Before that could

4

begin, two middle-aged women, one white and the other black, gestured to him. They agreed completely on what they had to say. While one of the robbers held a gun on the clerk, the other threatened the customers with a large handgun. As he herded them toward one side of the small store, he walked backward, slipped on something, and recovered his balance by snapping his left hand against the corner of a glass-topped showcase. They thought there might be fingerprints.

The sergeant acted on that immediately; he directed one of the agents on the scene to dust the corner of the case at once. The results were positive: A good set of prints was lifted by means of cellophane tape. That didn't make an identification certain, but it could be a great help. The chances were excellent that the suspect in question had been in custody and his prints would be on file. The new computer techniques for matching up prints, while not yet perfected, enormously speeded up the process, especially when a partial description of the suspect was available.

Lieutenant Dick Smith arrived on the scene to survey their progress. A house-to-house canvass was already going on; the occupants of every lighted home in the immediate area were being systematically interviewed to find out if they had seen or heard anything the least bit out of the ordinary. Because four dogs had barked when they normally would not have done so, and because one young man had been putting his bicycle into the garage at just the right time, the path that the bandits had taken on foot was retraced. One yard had been freshly watered and it yielded up several usable footprints.

By that time the approximate location where the bandits' car had been hidden was known. Officer Bob Watson was among those who were taking part in the investigation. Surveying the scene carefully, he determined the three or four most likely places where the car could have been left. He rang three doorbells and conducted three interviews without success, but he knew that police work, like the mills of the gods, consisted of grinding exceedingly fine.

When he rang the bell persistently at a house set back

5

from the sidewalk and showing no light, he was at last rewarded when Mrs. Ma'ellya Tilman framed herself in the doorway. She was a very large woman and not inclined to be sociable. She had been watching television in the back and the climax of the program was about to come. She had only torn herself away because a phalanx of commercials had come on.

"And what do *you* want?" she demanded. Officer Watson's uniform was clearly visible even in the poor light, but she was not impressed.

"I'd like to talk to you for a moment," Watson said. "May I come in?"

Heaving a great sigh to show how much she was being imposed upon, Mrs. Tilman reluctantly opened the screen door. Watson waited until she had gone back inside; her proportions were so ample that he had no choice.

The living room was sparsely furnished with two decrepit pieces that had once been part of a corner group. They had been jumped on and pounded into shapelessness. The once bright upholstery was stained and at the end of one piece it had been completely torn off.

Watson was not surprised; he had been in many low-income homes that were very similar regardless of who owned them. He appeared not to notice, but Mrs. Tilman still gave him a one-word explanation. "Children," she said.

Bob Watson remained standing in the middle of the small room.

"May I ask your name, please?" he began.

"Tilman, Mrs. Tilman." She looked about for a second as though she felt the need for further explanation; it was almost as if she had been caught at a disadvantageous moment and felt the pressure to justify herself. "I'm divorced," she added.

Watson was a good professional policeman: he nodded an acknowledgment but did not comment. He wasn't there for that purpose. "Mrs. Tilman, just a short while ago the grocery store at Fair Oaks and Hammond was robbed and the manager was badly hurt."

The huge woman pressed a hand across her chest. "I'm

6

glad I wasn't there," she said. "I go there all the time."

"Then you probably know the man who was injured—Mr. Raymond."

"I never asked the clerk his name."

"The point is, Mrs. Tilman, we're asking everyone in the neighborhood who might have seen anything to help us. We know that the suspects are two young black men, about eighteen to twenty-five, and dressed in dark clothing. We know that they fled on foot in this direction. They almost certainly left their car somewhere around here."

Mrs. Tilman was suspicious. "How come you're always blaming black men? Did anyone see them?"

"Yes, Mrs. Tilman, several people did. I'm afraid that there isn't any doubt about that. Now tell me, did you see anything at all that caught your attention about ten or fifteen minutes ago?"

Mrs. Tilman drew a deep breath and pretended to think. She looked again at Watson, then she unburdened herself. "I don't want anybody coming back here and giving me any trouble. You know what I mean."

Watson was immediately sympathetic. "Indeed I do. We never give out the names of people who help us if it can be avoided." He stopped there and waited.

"Well, I've called you people two or three times about the kids parking their cars in my driveway. I've never gotten no satisfaction. Tonight another car was left on my property. I didn't call because I can't get cooperation. The police are always too busy up in the rich areas."

"Please, can you describe the car?" Watson asked. He had his notebook ready.

"It was old and kind of banged up. Don't ask me what kind it was; I don't know. It was old, that's all."

"Would you say it was a sedan?"

"Just an old car, like I told you."

"Perhaps you noticed the color."

"How many times have I got to tell you…"

Watson caught that in midair. "I'm very sorry, Mrs. Tilman, I wasn't trying to press you. I don't suppose that you noticed any part of the license number?"

The huge woman put her arms across her waist and lifted her massive bosom as though she were striking a pose. "Of course I did!" she answered. "Now will you do something about it?"

Leonard "Piano" Tompkins, meanwhile, was having one of the best times of his life. He had had a number of drinks, he was flushed with the success of the robbery, his escape, and the certainty that he would never be caught. He had been in central jail twice and he knew that he was too smart, with all that he had learned, to ever go back to that pigs' hole again. At his home, two unmarked cars carefully parked in the shadows were patiently waiting for his return.

2

When Chief Robert McGowan, of the Pasadena Police Department, stepped out of the elevator into the lobby of the Hilton restaurant located on the top floor, manager Juan Ribot was waiting to welcome him. "Good afternoon, Chief McGowan," he said. "Always a pleasure to have you here. Your friends have arrived."

With that he led the way past the lavish buffet to a secluded corner table where two men in plain business suits were quietly waiting. As soon as the chief had seated himself, a hovering bar waiter closed in, took the drink order, and then just as quickly withdrew.

As soon as he was out of hearing, one of the two men introduced himself. He was sandy-haired, probably in his early forties, and obviously kept himself in shape. "Bill Conners, Chief McGowan," he said, and handed over his card. "This is Jim Reynolds."

Reynolds, who was dark-haired and quite slender, nodded but did not offer to shake hands. McGowan caught the fact at once that his luncheon companions wanted to attract as little attention as possible.

"We very much appreciate your coming," Reynolds said. "Particularly on such short notice."

"We're always glad to oblige the State Department," McGowan answered, speaking for his department more than for himself.

"Thank you." Reynolds hesitated; he was slightly older than his colleague and apparently a little more cautious.

"This is a very nice place—wonderful view. I only hope it isn't too public."

"Don't worry about that," McGowan replied. "The manager won't seat anyone else near us unless it becomes absolutely necessary."

Conners took some time to look out the window at the city below. "I like this," he said quite simply. It was obvious that he was marking time until the drinks were served.

"It's attractive, especially on a clear day like today," McGowan commented. "Sometimes we have a smog problem, but usually it's quite nice. We think it's a very good city to live in."

Reynolds looked into the chief's face carefully for a moment. "We know quite a lot about Pasadena," he said.

"Have you been studying up?" the chief asked.

"Yes, in a way." He looked up, saw the waiter coming, and stopped the conversation until the drinks had been put on the table. When the waiter had gone, McGowan came to the point. "Now what can we do for you?" he asked.

Reynolds tasted his drink, nodded his head a fraction in approval, then carefully looked around to assure himself once more that they would not be overheard.

"You understand that this is completely sub rosa," he said.

"Of course."

"Then let me ask you this: how much do you know about present-day Africa?"

"Not much more than what I read in the newspapers," McGowan answered. "It's a little far from our jurisdiction."

"Have you heard anything about Bakara?"* Reynolds asked.

"Not very much," McGowan said.

"It's one of the many new republican nations with a president and all that," Reynolds continued. "But it's of particular interest to us for a number of reasons. It has a strategic position directly in the path of communist expansion on the continent. It has one or two important natural re-

*A required pseudonym for the actual country involved.

10

sources; we'd like to buy the total supply of certain minerals that the country produces, but there's no need to go into that. Of greater concern at the moment is the fact that very recently the government there refused the offer of Cuban military 'advisers.' Before that, when the Russians tried to get in, they were politely told, 'thanks, but no thanks.'"

"Interesting," McGowan said. "Would you call the country pro-American?"

"Not necessarily, although we are pretty good friends—or are trying to be. Actually, the president is a man of real ability: he's seen what's happened to other nations that have fallen under communist rule and he doesn't want that for his people. Cambodia, in particular, impressed him. He's a very well-informed man."

Although Conners was apparently the younger of the two men, McGowan gathered that he was actually more important. That opinion was reinforced when Conners took up the conversation without any challenge from his companion. "When you speak about black African presidents, people instinctively think of Idi Amin rather than of Tubman or some others who are genuinely capable. Some of them are strongly Marxist, but that we have to live with while it lasts. President Motamboru of Bakara isn't."

"Have you met him?" the chief asked.

"On one or two occasions—one quite recently, as a matter of fact. At that time he asked us—the State Department, that is—for a considerable favor. It was heavy enough to go all the way to the White House."

"Was it approved there?"

"Yes."

The waiter approached at a discreet distance to see if more drinks were desired. McGowan shook his head very slightly and nodded toward the buffet. "Not that I wish to interrupt you," he said, "but the buffet is clear at the moment. I suggest that we get our plates."

"Good enough," Reynolds agreed.

Ten minutes later the three men returned with full plates to their table. Glasses of ice water had been set out

11

and Ribot was waiting to find out what beverages should be served. He saw to it that two coffees and an iced tea were quickly supplied, then nodded to McGowan and left. The large restaurant was gradually filling up, but no one had been seated anywhere within earshot of the chief's table.

McGowan broke off a piece of bread and buttered it. "Go on," he invited.

Reynolds glanced at his partner for a moment and then picked up the topic once more. "Within the past few weeks, President Motamboru has received several threats against his life. Serious ones. That's not unusual in that part of the world, but we happen to know that he has good reason to be concerned."

"You have intelligence reports?" the chief asked.

"Yes, we do. He turned down some people who don't take no for an answer—not if they can help it. He simply doesn't want *any* outside powers telling him how to run his own country. At the moment, his stand is very important to us."

"How popular is he with his own people?" McGowan asked.

"If he were to run for re-election tomorrow, he'd get more than 90 per cent of the vote. The people sense that he's honest and a genuine patriot—he's for Bakara. He helped to establish it as a nation and its future is his whole life right now. That and his family."

McGowan looked up from his plate at that moment and paused. "So that's it," he said.

Reynolds looked again toward Conners, clearly inviting him to fill in the rest.

The younger man put down his fork. "You've guessed it. President Motamboru is determined to stay where he is and carry on with his job. I've got to respect him for that. But you know what the guerilla and terrorist groups have been doing recently—hitting not only key people but also their families. That way they hope to create a greater impact—a greater fear in others."

"I take it that the president has asked to have his family

12

sheltered in this country," McGowan said. "Somebody hit on Pasadena, and that's where we are at the moment."

"Not quite," Conners said. "By the way, how is the man who was shot in the holdup last night making out?"

"He wasn't shot; he was pistol-whipped. He's going to need some dental work and plastic surgery, but otherwise he's all right. He took a bad smash in the face; fortunately his eyes weren't involved."

"Have you any suspects?"

McGowan hesitated for just a second. "This hasn't been released yet, but we have one suspect in custody and he's been positively identified by two reliable witnesses. We'll get his partner; it's only a matter of time. L.A.P.D. made the arrest in their jurisdiction and they know who the other man is. There's an APB out on him now."

"Good enough." By unexpressed consent the serious conversation stopped since there was good food to be eaten. McGowan welcomed the break; it gave him a chance to collect his thoughts and sort out some pieces of information his intelligence people had picked up.

When he was finally ready, Conners began again quite calmly. "In Washington we have a resources file that includes tens of thousands of individuals who have special capabilities. Many of them are government employees or officials who hold security clearances. A lot are in the armed forces; some are police officers. It's all computerized, so we can come up with the people we need very quickly if the need arises. Last week we needed a policeman, or someone like him, in Cleveland who could speak both Yugoslavian and Czech. We turned up a fireman sixty miles away who was born in Prague and who had married a Yugoslavian girl."

"Somehow," McGowan said, "I had the impression that the major language in Yugoslavia was Serbo-Croatian."

Reynolds looked at his partner and pursed his lips slightly.

Conners had the decency to flush. "All right—you have me there," he admitted. "A lesson learned. My apologies."

McGowan let the matter pass. "We have several hundred

very capable people, such as Terry Blumenthal, who is an exceptionally well-qualified pilot. Some of our personnel have language capabilities and other skills outside their work. But nobody in the department, to my knowledge, can qualify as an expert on Africa."

"That isn't what we're after," Reynolds said. "What we need is a man, specifically a black man, who is totally dependable and who might be available for a very sensitive assignment. He should also be a man of high intelligence."

"We have several people who meet those qualifications," McGowan declared, "but what you're saying is that you want Virgil Tibbs."

3

Although the setting sun had changed from a molten yellow to a dust-filtered red, the intense heat of the San Joaquin Valley still held the whole area south of Bakersfield in its stifling grip. Route 99 stretched taut and unrelieved across the semidesert terrain toward the south and the pale gray-brown shadows that were the beginning of the Sierra Madre Mountains.

At the wheel of his reasonably new air-conditioned Chevrolet, Virgil Tibbs held a steady road speed, pacing the rest of the automobile traffic at somewhere between sixty and sixty-five miles per hour. That was over the speed limit, but since he had left northern California he had seen very few cars doing less on the open highways. The heavy trucks—and there were a multitude of them—were going considerably faster.

He was not in a hurry. He was, in fact, coming home a day early from a week off, but he had finished what he had wanted to do up north and he could use the extra day in Pasadena attending to some personal business. Also, the idea of sleeping in after his long drive appealed to him very much.

Despite the late afternoon heat, he left his window open so that he could feel the rush of air and look out at the panorama of irrigated fields. And Virgil enjoyed driving, even if he was only going back to his empty apartment.

The air conditioning was doing a satisfactory job of keeping him cool despite the open window. He was at that

15

moment a completely free man and the sensation of it filled him in a way he would never have admitted in public. He still vividly remembered his boyhood in the Deep South and the scars that had been burned into him when he had first learned that he was "colored." In the beginning he had known no hope, as his father had known none, but then things had changed and he had fought his hard battle to climb out of the restricted environment into which he had been born. Finally the day had come when, in cap and gown, he had received his degree and had officially become an educated man.

Not long after that he had been accepted as a police trainee. The rest was a matter of record in the venerable building that housed the Pasadena Police Department.

The superhighway made its long descent and opened up into a maze of freeways. He took the Golden State, which cut diagonally across the San Fernando Valley toward Glendale and the intersection with the 210 Freeway, which in turn ran directly eastward into Pasadena. Driving became mechanical then, purged of its enjoyment by the overfamiliarity of the unending freeways.

Virgil drove through Glendale with the comforting realization that he was on the last lap. He climbed with the freeway up through Eagle Rock and then turned off at Orange Grove Avenue. Eight minutes later he backed with practiced ease into his assigned parking spot, carried his bag up two flights of stairs, and stood at last in front of his own door.

He slipped his key into the lock with a sense of finality, opened the door, and snapped on the light. Then he stood perfectly still, looking and listening. He had often wondered if he would ever come home and find that he had been burgled, but what confronted him far exceeded that. His apartment was completely empty except for the carpeting that had come with the place and the drapes, which were still drawn across the windows.

He set his bag down and thought very fast. He was almost certain that he hadn't entered the wrong apartment; he soon eliminated that possibility by checking the number on the door. It was the right one, 27, and the numbers had not been changed recently. Looking carefully at the left-hand wall of his living room where the nude study by William Holt-Rymers had hung, he could see the faint outline of where it had been.

There was no point in being quiet since he had announced himself by turning on the light, but Virgil still slipped his gun into his hand as he checked the bedroom and the kitchen. The bedroom was completely bare and the closet empty. In the kitchen he found only two or three packages of food that had been opened for some time and had apparently not been considered worth carting away.

The telephone was resting on the floor, still connected to a wall box. He picked it up, listened for a dial tone, and discovered that the line was dead. With that added piece of information, he began to reason. He could have been cleaned out by burglars with a van. Things like that had happened before. Someone had once stolen fifty thousand cobblestones from a public street. Although, like most policemen, he didn't publicize his home address or his phone number, and although his car was registered with the police department, someone interested enough could have found out that he was out of town. The trip had by no means been a secret.

But burglars wouldn't have bothered having the phone disconnected. That was what didn't fit. Also, burglars who completely stripped homes or apartments left behind things they considered of no value. Apart from the food, nothing had been discarded; the place was bare.

Still looking about him, Virgil noted one more thing: It was impossible to move out without creating some dust and litter. The apartment had been carefully cleaned, as though it was being readied to be re-rented. He made a mental check and distinctly remembered that he had paid the rent on time before leaving. And there was no way that a judgment could have been declared against him and his property removed as a consequence.

He turned off the light, bag in hand, closed the door behind him, and went down to the manager's apartment.

It was closed and dark—no one was at home. Tired, but his mind still working, he went back down to his car and was slightly relieved to see that it was still where he had left it a few minutes before. He unlocked it once again, got behind the wheel, and drove to the Pasadena Police Station. He parked across the street to keep the fifteen-minute spaces clear, then walked back across the street and into the lobby.

The two uniformed girls behind the counter looked up and the blonde greeted him. "Hello, Virg; back already?"

"Yes, I'm back," Tibbs answered. "Now I'd like to find out what's going on."

"It's a pretty quiet night, we had a couple of four fifteens..." She stopped when she saw his face. "Oh, I remember now. We got the word that if you came in, you should see the watch commander."

"Who's on duty?"

"Lieutenant Robenson."

"Buzz me in."

Tibbs passed through the electrically controlled doorway into the long corridor that ran the length of the building. Three quarters of the way down he walked into the open door of the watch commander's office without invitation. "Hello, Jim," he said to the man behind the desk.

Lieutenant James Robenson, who shared Tibbs' heritage and was proud of it, looked up quickly. A slightly artificial smile came to his lips as he waved Tibbs toward a chair. "Welcome back, Virg. Have a nice trip?"

"Up until about twenty minutes ago. Now what the hell is going on?"

Robenson shook his head. "We haven't had a decent homicide since you've been gone, not even a two eleven."*

"I'm about to commit one unless I get some answers."

The watch commander opened the middle drawer of his desk and took out an envelope. "You're early, you know that. Diane Stone left this here for you in the event you showed up."

*Armed robbery.

18

Virgil didn't need to be reminded that Mrs. Stone was the chief's secretary.

He took the envelope, tore it open, and found a small typed slip inside.

Mr. Tibbs:
If you return home before we have a chance to talk to you, please call 000-0000.*

Virgil reached across the desk, then thought better of using the watch commander's phone: An urgent call could come in at any time. He went across the hall, where he had complete privacy, and dialed the number, one that he did not recall ever having seen before. After the second ring it was answered, and Virgil at once recognized the chief's voice.

"Good evening, Chief McGowan, this is Virgil Tibbs."

"Oh yes, Virgil; you're back early, aren't you?"

"Yes, I just came over from home. Only it doesn't seem to be home anymore."

"I know. We tried to reach you, but you had checked out sooner than we expected."

"I see."

"I'm sorry, Virgil, if you've been inconvenienced."

"A little surprised, perhaps."

"I can certainly understand that. Now, have you told anyone, either a civilian or anyone within the department, what you found?"

"No, but I was about to discuss the matter with Jim Robenson."

"I'd prefer that you didn't. Don't talk to anyone except me. That's a firm order."

"Yes, sir. Since we're on an open line..."

"I have that in mind," the chief cut in. "There's a note for you down in the com center. I'll see you in my office tomorrow morning at nine-thirty."

"Yes, sir," Tibbs replied, and hung up. Some questions had been answered, but a lot more were in his mind as he

*Deleted by request.

went down the stairs and through the underground passageways that led to the communications center. He did not ordinarily have much occasion to go there; it was a carefully secured area that was in operation twenty-four hours every day. When he got to the doorway, he picked up the phone, identified himself, and then held up his badge where it could be seen through the one-way glass.

As soon as the lock clicked, he went inside the large, quiet, carpeted room where the two police dispatch consoles were manned by highly capable young women. "I understand that there is a message for me here," Tibbs said.

One of the dispatchers promptly handed him an envelope with his name and badge number written on the front. "I hope it's not bad news," she said.

"So do I," Tibbs acknowledged. "Thank you." He left the com center and didn't open the envelope until he was alone in a long, cylindrical passageway that was heavily stocked with emergency food supplies and medical equipment. He had never gone through a rigmarole like this since he had joined the department. He knew that Chief McGowan did not go in for unnecessary dramatics; if all these precautions had been taken, there had to be a very good reason.

The envelope contained a slip of paper with the chief's name at the top. He was instructed, upon receipt of the message, to go immediately to an address that was supplied. Virgil knew the city well; he'd had to learn every street and byway when he had been on patrol. If a code three call reached him, there would be no time to look at maps or city directories. The address was on the east side of town and up in the hills. Most of the homes in that area were elaborate and expensive; it was one of the choice neighborhoods in the city.

Tibbs put the slip carefully into his wallet. He climbed back up the stairs, went out through the rear door, and got back into his car. As he fitted the key into the ignition, he had a strong feeling that the day he had thought was all but over might be stretching into a very long night.

He drove eastward on Colorado Boulevard, drawing certain conclusions as he rode. Whoever had cleaned out his apartment had done so with the knowledge and approval of the chief himself. That ruled out burglary. If the manager had been home, she would probably have had a message for him too.

The most likely explanation was that he was in some kind of acute personal danger, something serious enough that the department was prepared to hide him for as long as might be necessary. That was pretty extreme, but it fit all the facts. Another point was the fact that the chief himself had given him his instructions, not one of the commanders or, as would have been proper, the head of his own section.

A patrol unit went past, headed in the other direction. The two officers apparently didn't see him, and he didn't wave, as he would ordinarily have done. There was almost no traffic behind him and he wasn't being followed.

Obviously, he was not walking into any kind of a setup since the source of his instructions was beyond question. As he neared the eastern end of Colorado Boulevard, he turned north and soon was weaving his way up the twisting streets that climbed through the foothills. Elaborate mansions began to appear, as well as some smaller houses that had been built before the area had become both fashionable and expensive.

Virgil had developed a full set of police instincts while he had been on patrol; they told him that the whole neighborhood was peaceful and that all the cars he saw parked belonged where they were. He turned into a smaller cross street that ended in a loop. Four houses had been built there, two with panoramic views of the city below, two others on more modest lots that backed against the hillside. The number he had been given was one of those.

He got out of his car, walked up to the door, and rang the bell. There were lights on inside and he could hear the sounds of a TV set. There was not a thing to suggest to him, an experienced policeman, that there was anything at all wrong.

The door was opened, a little carefully, and a young

21

woman stood there. As far as Tibbs knew, he had never seen her before. Her age could have been anywhere between twenty-five and forty; it was not easy to tell. Her poise at once indicated breeding as she kept one hand on the doorknob, waiting to see what he wanted. She was dressed very simply in a deep blue skirt and a white blouse that set off the dark richness of her skin.

A sudden flash came to Virgil, an idea that had been forming in his mind almost without his knowledge. He got it just in time; a second or two more would have been too late. "Is this Mr. Tibbs's residence?" he asked.

"Yes it is," the young woman answered. Her voice was well modulated, with just a faint trace of an accent. "I'm sorry, but he isn't at home."

A small boy, who might have been eight, stood half hidden behind the woman, who was evidently his mother. He looked out from behind her with grave, inquiring eyes.

"Excuse me," Virgil said, "but are you..."

He did not need to finish the sentence; she cut him short with a nod of her head. "I am Mrs. Tibbs," she said quietly. "Would you like to leave a message? I'll be glad to give it to my husband when he returns."

Tibbs took out his wallet and handed her a card that displayed the blue seal of the Pasadena Police Department in the upper-left-hand corner. Then he stood quite still and waited for her reaction.

She was superbly poised, he had to give her that; she didn't turn a hair as she read the card. Then she held the door open a little wider and said, "Please come in."

Tibbs crossed the threshold into a small foyer. To his left was a sizable, richly carpeted living room, tastefully and expensively furnished. The only thing he recognized was his Holt-Rymers painting, which hung over the fireplace.

During the next few seconds, a little girl appeared; she was darker-skinned than either her mother or the boy, whom Tibbs assumed was her brother. "Hello," she said, and waited. The single word told Virgil something about her: English was not her native tongue.

22

He looked at the painting for a moment and then asked, conversationally, "Are any of my other things here?"

He had to admire the way the young woman fielded that question. "I believe that everything else is," she answered, matching his composure precisely. "I'm afraid we did use a can or two of soup, and I haven't had a chance to get to the market to replace them."

Virgil's thoughts were racing. He stood there, sorting out the ideas and possibilities that were flashing through his mind, when the telephone rang.

The young woman picked it up and answered. She listened a moment and then said, "Yes, he just arrived. I wasn't expecting him or I would have had something ready." After another pause she added, "No, no trouble at all. Thank you. Good-bye." She put the phone down.

"Was that Chief McGowan?" Virgil asked.

"No, it wasn't."

That was fresh evidence that he needed a moment or two to digest these events. He looked carefully once more at the young woman who had just claimed to be his wife and watched her every reaction as he spoke.

"I believe that this has gone far enough," he said. "I was given this address and I came here under orders. I know that this isn't any kind of a con game or an attempt to embarrass me. I have to assume that it is all right and proper. But I haven't been briefed—I don't know what this is all about. Now I'd like to be informed."

He heard a footstep behind him and whirled around on the balls of his feet; his weapon was in his hand before he had finished turning. When he saw who the newcomer was, he put his gun back and visibly relaxed.

The man who had come up behind him was about Virgil's age, a little shorter and of more stocky build. He was simply dressed in a dark business suit and an undistinguished tie. His distinctly Oriental features, accented by the glasses he wore, were deceptively bland and open. It was one of his major assets that he did not look at all like a policeman. His name was Bob Nakamura and he was Tibbs's partner.

"Put the iron away, Virg, you might scare your kids," Bob said like the Rotarian he was. "Now if you'll sit down, beside your wife if you'd like, I'll tell you what this is all about."

4

Tibbs did sit down, characteristically noting that the chair he'd chosen was very comfortable. He was glad that it was; any relaxation that it could provide was welcome.

Bob sat down too; as he did so, any suggestion of bantering left him. The way he sat, with his elbows resting on his knees so that he was leaning slightly forward, told Tibbs that he was about to be deadly serious.

"You may have wondered how come you got a week off so suddenly. I know you've had a request in for some time; that simply made it more convenient."

Virgil nodded and waited.

"You were not supposed to get back until tomorrow. The machinery was all set up to reach you up north before you left and to tell you to come directly in before you went home. When the word came in that you had left early, the boss set up the backup plan. He was sure that you wouldn't go off half-cocked when you found your apartment empty. You never do."

"I never found my apartment empty before," Virgil said.

"All right, but you know what I mean. Now understand, Virg, that this is damned serious; hence the runaround you got. Security is as tight as we can make it. The chief knows, I know, and you're about to know. That's all. Not even Deputy Chief Winders has been briefed. Does that give you a clue?"

"Yes, it does."

Bob Nakamura folded his hands between his knees as if

to remind himself of the seriousness of the situation. "I'm in on this, Virg, only because we're partners and the chief felt that I might notice too much and ask some questions around the shop. So he decided, very reluctantly, that I'd have to be briefed. It's a good thing, in a way, because I've been covering for you."

"Bodyguard?" Tibbs asked.

Bob nodded. "You knew perfectly well that I wouldn't be here, and at this hour, unless it was a question of duty. Not very long ago the chief was approached by the State Department on a top-security matter. The lady whom you have just met is Mrs. Motamboru. Does the name ring a bell?"

"It's an African name," Tibbs answered. "She's exceptionally poised and obviously well educated, but I did note that she speaks with a slight accent. The little girl's accent is much more noticeable. I thought at first that they were members of a French family; the accent seemed to fit."

The young woman spoke for the first time since they had sat down. "You're very perceptive, Mr. Tibbs. French is my second language."

"English is your third language, then?" Virgil asked. He was definitely impressed.

"Yes, English, or possibly German."

"And you were principally educated in France?"

"I took my doctorate there—at the Sorbonne."

Virgil looked at his partner. "This lady is obviously the wife of a very highly placed man."

Bob nodded gravely. "That's the easiest deduction you ever made."

"Wait a minute," Tibbs said. "I had a chance to catch up a little on world events while I was gone." He turned to his hostess. "Madam, is your husband the president of Bakara?"

When she nodded slowly, Tibbs sat back in his chair, a little stunned. "I get it now. Of course. Bakara is having a fierce guerilla problem. People have been killed. I don't know who's inciting it, but I do remember reading about it. The president wanted his family out, in a place of safety. We got the nod."

"That's most of it," Bob confirmed, "but there's a little more. Bakara is, you could say, strategic. The Russians have a stake in Africa; so do the Chicoms. Even the Cubans have gotten into the act. President Motamboru doesn't want any part of them, or anybody else, interfering with the development of his country except on an invitational basis. *If* some of the international powers that don't like his attitude could locate his family..."

"I don't need the melodrama to see it," Virgil said. "Now that I have that much, I think I see my part. I've been with the department for some time and I've saved my money. Now I've bought a home here, in a very nice neighborhood, for myself and my family. It's at the end of the road, so there are only three sets of neighbors who are likely to pay us any attention at all."

"Two," Bob corrected. "The house next door is still unsold. Both the other families have been thoroughly checked out without their knowledge. You have a physicist at Cal. Tech. and a surgeon who is on a very irregular schedule. He lectures and teaches as well as operates. Neither family is at all likely to take too much interest in you and yours. They're nice people, but they're intensely busy."

"I do have a few friends," Tibbs said, thinking carefully. "It's unlikely, but if my new neighbors were to mention my name, it's possible that they might do so to someone who knows me. And knows that I'm not married."

"The chief thought of that," Bob said. "You first met this lady when you were in Nepal on the Doris Friedkin case. She is the ex-wife of a French merchant. She has independent means and was traveling when you met her at the hotel where you both were staying. In the casino, if anyone asks you. I won't suggest that it was on the bounce, but you did manage to engage her interest while you were both there."

"Then the children are hers by a previous marriage."

"Exactly—which explains why they speak differently than you do."

Tibbs sat very still and thought for a few moments. When he looked up, he addressed himself to the lady who was present. "Madam, it's obvious that you have given your consent to all this or you would not be here."

She nodded. "That's correct," she said.

"Does your husband know where you are?"

"Not the exact address; he did not want any document in the country that would reveal where we were. He does know that we are on the West Coast, in a comfortable home provided by your State Department, and that an American policeman of irreproachable reputation has been assigned to protect us and to pose as my husband."

"It's quite obvious," Tibbs continued, "that in order to play the role of your husband I would have to live here. It seems that I have already moved in. If the story is ever made public, there could be an adverse effect on your reputation."

Mrs. Motamboru folded her hands across her knees and looked at him quite calmly. "That is a considered risk I am quite willing to take. I have never in my life been at all concerned about what people might say. I do not depend on small minds."

Virgil relaxed. "I'm sure we can work out some kind of an arrangement so that I am the least possible bother to you," he said.

"I have a suggestion, Mr. Tibbs, if I may."

"By all means, madam."

"No one knows how long this may last—how long you will have to put up with us. Since I have been told quite a lot about you, and I have reason to trust you entirely, I think it best that you do act for the time being as head of the family and as a temporary father to my children."

She smoothed her skirt with her hands, giving Tibbs the first indication that she was at all disturbed. "With a single obvious exception, the more you choose to play the role of husband and father, the better I believe it will be."

"That's it," Bob Nakamura said.

"I'll still go to work every day."

"Of course," his partner answered.

"While I'm gone, who will look after this family?"

"I don't know all the details," Bob answered. "Obviously they're depending a lot on airtight security. There's also a federal agency that will have this house under surveillance on some sort of a schedule. Beyond that, you'd better talk to the chief."

"I have an appointment with him in the morning."

"Good. I'm about to split, so have a nice night in your new home. By the way, I put all your things in your room and most of your furniture in the family room. You've got your own bath and your clothes are all hung in your closet. And don't worry that the movers may talk; that's all been covered."

Bob said his proper good-nights and left. When the door closed behind him, Virgil had his first full realization of the situation in which he found himself.

His new wife came over to him. "One thing we forgot to tell you," she said. "My children have been carefully tutored for this. They're still very young, but I don't think they'll make any bad mistakes. If they do, it will probably be attributed to the fact that they are not yet used to having a new father."

"Which is certainly true," Tibbs said.

"Now, I know how tired you must be, but we should talk for a while, if you don't mind. My name is Miriam and I think it best that you use it. I shall call you Virgil. Now if you will come out to the kitchen, I will prepare a late supper for you."

For the first time she dropped her restrained formality and smiled quite pleasantly. "You are getting one bonus out of this rather bewildering arrangement," she said. "As it happens, I'm a very good cook."

Chief McGowan seemed almost amused. He shut the door of his office promptly at nine-thirty, after having instructed Mrs. Stone that he was not to be disturbed except in case of emergency. Both of them knew that there was a phone on the chief's desk with a very restricted number; the few people who knew it could call him directly if necessary.

The chief did not sit down behind his desk; instead, he sat on one of the more comfortable upholstered chairs in the corner of his office so he could talk to Virgil Tibbs with a minimum of formality. "One thing I have to ask you," he began. "Are you willing to volunteer for this assignment?"

"Of course," Tibbs said.

"I hope that it won't last more than a week of two, but you understand that it could be longer."

"I think, sir," Tibbs answered, "that, based on what I know, it could go on for some time."

The chief crossed his legs and leaned back. "She's a very attractive woman," he said.

"I noticed that."

"I assume you can handle it."

"Considering who she is, the first tiny step that I take out of line will mean that I will have let you down, I will have let the State Department down, and I will be looking for work."

"I couldn't put it better myself," McGowan agreed.

"Now I'm going to damage your reputation a little," the chief continued after a few moments. "I know that things have a way of getting out, and accidents do happen. So if it does come to light anywhere in the department that you are living with a new family, you intend to marry the lady, but her divorce won't be final for a little while longer. Meanwhile you have set up housekeeping."

"I know a lot of very good cops who have roommates."

"So you won't be conspicuous, and you have a ready-made excuse for not inviting any of your friends over. She isn't quite ready to acknowledge that she's living with you."

"Somebody has thought this out very carefully," Tibbs said.

"Thank you." The chief took up another subject. "We've been having a rash of particularly vicious armed robberies lately," he said. "A bad one went down just after you left. I'd like to have you sharpen your contacts, particularly in the black community, and see what you can find out."

"Yes, sir," Tibbs said.

"While you're on this special assignment, I want you to go through proper channels on all your regular work, but keep me informed of anything you feel I should know. You're authorized direct contact, and you have my home number. Don't talk to anyone else, no matter what credentials he offers, until I've cleared it personally."

The phone rang. McGowan answered it, listened, and then asked a question or two. When he had completed a brief conversation, he hung up and turned toward Tibbs.

"You can go back to work now," he said. "We've just had a homicide and this one isn't a domestic walk-through. Check in at your office and let them send you out from there."

Tibbs got up quickly and put his hand on the doorknob. He started to say something appropriate when the chief added, "I know that you seem to relish oddball situations, Virgil, so this one should suit you just fine."

5

Officer Jim Riley, who had discovered the body, was waiting at the scene when Virgil arrived. So were three other uniformed policemen who were fully aware that if the word got out they might have a problem keeping people away, even though it was indoors.

The shedlike building was laid out on a north-south axis. High along the east wall was a balcony to accommodate spectators, who could always be depended upon to show up by the hundreds just before the Tournament of Roses. The facility was principally used as a site for decorating some of the highly elaborate parade floats that would roll down Colorado Boulevard on New Year's Day.

In a two-hundred-man department there are few strangers. Tibbs knew Riley and saw at once that he was primed with information. As Virgil approached him, the patrolman met him halfway.

After they had exchanged nods, Riley reported. "I got a suspicious circumstances call and responded." He gestured toward the body that lay stretched out on the floor. "When I came in, I found him hanging from the balcony. The rope was around his neck and he was motionless. I called for a paramedic team and then cut him down as fast as I could, under the assumption that he might still be alive."

"The only thing to do," Tibbs agreed. "Did you try mouth-to-mouth resuscitation?"

"Yes, and it wasn't pleasant: He was cold enough for me to know that he had been dead for some time. The paramedics got here fast and relieved me. They determined that he was clinically dead, so we laid him out on the floor and called for the homicide team."

As he spoke, three other members of the department, some carrying equipment, came into the shed. They went to work without delay while Tibbs checked with the other uniformed men. None of them had anything more to contribute to what had already been said.

"Has the body been IDed?" Virgil asked.

"No," Riley answered. "His pockets were empty. There's nothing on him to say who he was."

Tibbs pressed his lips together, sensing that he might have to do things the hard way. If it came to that, Bob Nakamura would help him out, but unless they had luck on their side, it could be a long and difficult road.

The deceased was a male Negro somewhere between eighteen and twenty-five years of age. The build and height were normal. His clothes consisted of a pair of well-worn cheap slacks held in place by a leather belt that had been used until the surface had largely peeled away. His shirt was a common work blue, with no distinguishing features whatever. Only his shoes were fairly new, but they had already begun to give way where the little toe on each foot pressed against the sides. They had not been well made or properly fitted. The deceased's hair was cut in a semi-Afro that had been fluffed to make his head appear larger.

All of which told Virgil Tibbs that the victim was almost identical in appearance to literally thousands of others who lived all over the Los Angeles basin. Only this one had been hanged and his pockets had been carefully emptied. If he had worn any sort of decoration around his neck, that too had been removed.

Tibbs took off his coat and laid it to one side. Then he began his detailed examination of the corpse. He flexed the fingers, removed the shoes, and flexed the feet. He looked into the victim's mouth for evidence of dental work. After that he gave his full attention to the neck area and to the section of rope that was still in place around it. He noted at once that the classic hangman's knot had not been used; instead, the end of the rope had been fitted with an eyelet. The stock had been run through it to form the noose. As a consequence, when the body had been cut down the tight grip of the rope around the neck had been loosened and it lay relatively free. The marks where it had ripped into the flesh were all too clear; it had not been a pleasant death.

Virgil examined the clothing as carefully as he could without removing it from the body. He opened the fly of the trousers and found that the victim had been wearing boxer-type nylon shorts of good quality; they had been freshly laundered. The socks, which were of the fancy ribbed variety, had an unpleasant odor; the right one had been darned at the heel. The shoes bore the label of a large discount chain with dozens of outlets in the area; tracing them would therefore be a virtual impossibility.

When he had at last finished, Tibbs got to his feet and, in the absence of an available washroom, wiped his hands on a clean handkerchief. His timing was unexpectedly good: Two men from the Los Angeles County Coroner's Office appeared with their carrier to take the body away. "You can have him," Virgil said. "I'll phone down later if I need any special work-ups."

The four uniformed policemen, who were still on hand, were ready to disperse. Riley lingered for a moment, interested. "Have you got anything?" he asked.

"Yes, I think so," Tibbs answered. "Some things are fairly obvious and I can do some educated guessing on one or two other points."

"Go ahead."

"All right. The deceased was a member of a fairly large family and he was a younger son. I don't think he was married—I'm pretty sure of that—and he lived with his mother. She, apparently, is a good woman who did the best she could for her son despite the fact that she has very limited financial resources. The victim did not commit suicide: He was definitely murdered by someone of better than average education who is probably a fairly voracious reader. To get back to the deceased, he was in all proba-

34

bility unemployed and I think it quite likely that he has a record. We may make him on prints or through a missing persons report. He's not a drifter, he has a regular home, and he will be missed. In fact, the report may already be in."

"You wouldn't care to tell me how he voted in the last election," Riley suggested.

"I don't think he did: He would have been too young. If he did vote, I would doubt that he went for the straight Republican ticket."

"Level with me, Virg, do you know him?"

"To the best of my knowledge, no."

Riley had clearly been on the point of leaving, but he seemed to have changed his mind. He walked up and down the shed for three or four minutes, thinking. Then he went back to talk to Tibbs once more.

"Let's go into it a little," he suggested. "I've got to write the report." That was a subterfuge, but it legitimized the question to a degree.

"Let's start with his belt," Tibbs began. "It was very well worn. The deceased was fairly slender, which is characteristic of young men of his age, but some of the holes showed signs of wear three or four notches out from where he normally fastened it."

"So it was a hand-me-down."

"Unless he bought it secondhand, but that doesn't figure. Belts don't cost that much new and it was already in tough shape before he started wearing it. So much so that I don't think it would even have been a charity handout."

"I see where you get the younger brother angle, but it could have been handed down by his father."

"I forgot to tell you: I doubt if he had one—at home, I mean. You saw the belt; it wasn't the kind that a man old enough to have been his father would normally choose. That is only a guess, but I think it's a probability."

"What about his mother?" Riley prompted.

"Well, that part's fairly easy. His socks and his underwear were definitely of much better quality than the rest of his clothing. One of his socks was neatly darned. Not

many young women today would know how to do that—
nor would bother."

"But a mother would, especially if she were an older
woman."

Tibbs nodded. "Exactly. And if she is an older woman,
that strengthens the idea that the victim was one of her
younger children. I see her as a lady of fifty-five or even
sixty. Two will get you five that the socks were a present
from her; I doubt that he would buy that quality for himself, judging by the rest of his clothes."

"No bet," Riley said.

"Another thing, Jim: The deceased didn't take very good
care of himself. His feet smelled and there wasn't much
evidence of cleanliness. The dirt was packed solidly under
his fingernails. But he was wearing good-quality nylon
shorts that had been freshly washed *and ironed.*"

"Mama," Riley noted.

"Mama," Tibbs agreed. "A mama who loved her son and
who tried to look after him. A wife who slept with him
would have wanted to see him cleaner, and would have
been in a position to insist on it. And, as I said, most young
women today can't darn."

"And there was no wedding ring," Riley added. "Of
course, not all married men wear one, and this man's pockets were emptied, so if he had a ring, it could have been
taken off."

"A wedding ring, even for women, is only significant if
it's present," Tibbs said. "The fact that the body didn't
have one supports the no-wife theory, but that's all."

"That's all I meant," Riley said.

"Good enough. If you looked at his hands, Jim, you
would have seen that he had very dirty nails, as I said, but
the flesh of his palms was very soft. So he wasn't a laborer
or workman who uses his hands. His clothing and his lack
of personal cleanliness pretty much rules out an office
worker or a salesman. Conclusion: unemployed."

"And mama doesn't have much money or she would have
seen her son better dressed," Riley continued. "From what

she had, she bought him respectable socks and some underwear."

Virgil nodded. "You know as well as I do that a lot of young people run around without any underwear. Mama saw to it that her son wore what she considered proper. Are you beginning to get a picture of her?"

"You said a few things about the murderer, Virg," Riley reminded him.

Tibbs heard him, but he had his lips pursed and was clearly thinking. "There's a lot to be learned from the way he was strung up," he said. Then, without any further comment, he left the premises. But he did not go back to police headquarters, where he knew he had work to do; instead he went first to the library.

6

By three that afternoon Virgil Tibbs already had most of the preliminary data concerning the homicide of the unknown young black on his desk. There was nothing whatever to indicate who might have committed the crime. The balcony had yielded no useful information, no prints had come up that held any hope of identifying the killer, and the rope itself was of a totally common variety. Furthermore, a little checking showed that it would be no problem at all to buy such a rope with an eyelet set at the end.

The one piece of additional information that the rope yielded was negative: It was fairly old and therefore any hope of tracking its purchaser was out the window. The hands of the victim had been tied behind his back by another length of clothesline, the kind sold in almost every supermarket and hardware store. It seemed to be a case of waiting to find out who the victim was and then tracing back from there.

When Bob Nakamura came in, Tibbs welcomed the chance to talk with him. They worked very well together and Bob's fertile mind frequently came up with some very good ideas. Bob closed the door, sat down, and then asked, "How did it go with your new family last night?"

"Pretty well, all things considered. Miriam made it very easy for me. I was introduced to the children as their temporary father. We spent enought time together to put them at ease, then she hustled them off to bed. They were no bother at all."

"And your temporary wife?"

"As a first impression, she's a winner all the way. Her husband is a man to be envied. She fixed me something to eat, and I didn't have to do the dishes afterward."

"If the water ever gets deep, Virg, let me know and I'll do what I can. I've been installed as a friend of the family, so I can call at any time."

"I won't forget," Tibbs promised. "Now I have a fresh homicide to add to my other duties."

"I heard about it; a young John Doe, black."

"So far almost nothing to go on, but we should be able to ID him fairly fast."

The phone rang. Tibbs picked it up and found that he was talking with a member of the intelligence unit. "We have a make on your homicide this morning," the caller said. "L.A.P.D. was running his prints when a missing persons call came in. They matched the body's prints with the file card on the missing person and bingo."

"Fine," Tibbs said. "Let me have it."

"The deceased was Leonard no-middle-name Tompkins, aged nineteen, residing in south central Los Angeles: I have the address. But get this: He was one of the two men who pulled the two eleven just after you left."

"I don't get it," Tibbs said. "If he was made for that two eleven hardly a week ago, what was he doing out of jail?"

"At the arraignment Judge Peabody, or Peabrain if you prefer, set a low bail because of some technicality. I don't know how he made it, but he did."

"Probably his family put up the security for his bond."

"Sounds likely. Tompkins had a considerable record beginning when he was twelve. He was in trouble most of the time."

Tibbs was busy taking notes. "Have we made his partner yet on that heist?"

"Yes. His name's Willie Leonard and he's on parole from the joint on the same charge. He's twenty-one and already has a long record of crimes with violence. He's being held in central jail."

"Has he copped out?"

"Not yet, but we have some good witnesses and they aren't afraid to finger the Adam Henry. The clerk who was hurt will also testify, so maybe this time they'll keep him for a while."

"God, I hope so," Tibbs said. "Have the next of kin been notified?"

"They probably know by now. Incidentally, Tompkins was a known PCP user, so add that to your bag."

"I will. Now let me have the address."

When he had hung up, Virgil turned to his partner and filled him in. "There's something here that doesn't add up," he said. "Tompkins was a punk who came out here with his partner to make a hit. Then they went back to L.A., where they were busted. What I want to know is: How come he shows up as a stiff back in our jurisdiction?"

"That's not too hard to figure," Bob answered. "He might have had a girl friend here and came out to see her. On a previous visit he cased the market and decided that it was good for a hit. I'll give you another one: He has some friends here. It's a good bet that he met them in jail. They might even have pointed him toward the market, which they couldn't hit themselves because they were known there."

Tibbs thought for a moment. "The girl idea isn't bad except that he was hardly in a condition to go calling; he wasn't clean and he smelled. The friends angle might work out, but I can't see them killing him."

"Not the way that he died. A knife or a gun would have been much more likely if someone in the black community wanted to get rid of him."

"I think I'll go and see his mother," Tibbs said. "Meanwhile, I've got a little theory of my own. Can you give me a hand?"

"Sure. What's on your mind?"

"There's been a lot of heat lately on some of the courts and judges for being too lenient with hard-core offenders. And the parole system is being widely criticized for releasing too many inmates who served only a small part of their sentences. Tompkins' partner was on parole and we know that Tompkins himself had a heavy record."

"You're thinking of crackpot crusaders?"

"Something like that. See what you can find regarding hard-nosed individuals or organizations. Also the KKK kind of bigot who might have it in for blacks."

"I'll do that," Bob promised.

The house in south central Los Angeles was set on a cross street devoid of shade trees or any other pretensions to beauty. The tiny houses were packed closely together, erected by a builder who comforted himself with the sure knowledge that he would never have to live in any of them. Few of them were as large as a thousand square feet, yet some of them had neat little lawns and were decorated with trimmed shrubs. The sidewalks on each side of the street were full of children; bicycles and skateboards were scattered about carelessly. There was not a white face to be seen anywhere.

Virgil Tibbs parked his unmarked car in front of a very modest dwelling that was desperately in need of paint. The tiny porch sagged dangerously on one side, but there were presentable curtains hung in the single front window. There was a doorbell, but it was hanging by two thin wires and quite clearly was not working. Tibbs knocked on the door.

The woman who opened it was of medium-heavy build. Her house dress was of the cheapest kind, but it was clean and neat. She held a handkerchief in her hand and it was painfully evident that she had been crying. "Yes?" she asked and with that single word betrayed her origin in the South.

"Mrs. Tompkins, I'm very sorry to disturb you at a time like this. I'm Mr. Tibbs of the Pasadena Police."

"Mr. Tibbs. I see." The woman stood silent and still for a few seconds as if hoping that some angel would come to relieve her of her burden. Then, with slow resignation, she held the door open wider. "Come in, Mr. Tibbs. I'm

41

'shamed to talk to you. I'm 'shamed you have to come here." Her eyes began to water and she wiped them with her already wet handkerchief.

Virgil walked directly into a tiny, sparsely furnished living room. What there was was very old and faded, but it was clean. Bits of white lace tried bravely to disguise the worn-out fabric on the arms of the single upholstered chair. The plain wooden table had been polished and the cheap ceramic figure of a geisha girl that adorned it was dust-free. A plastic-covered guitar case stood in one corner.

The woman who had let him in walked as though her feet hurt her with every step, but she remained on them until her guest had been offered, and had accepted, the one chair that promised a modicum of comfort. After that she sank into a metal folding chair that she overflowed on each side. Tibbs had already evaluated her and, despite his long experience as a policeman, his heart ached for her.

"Mrs. Tompkins," he began carefully, "I want you to know that I didn't come here to add to your sorrow in any way."

When her eyes teared again, he pulled out his own clean handkerchief and offered it to her. She accepted it and as she took it into her hands a tiny bridge was built between them. He waited while she gathered herself together and was able at last to face him.

"Did the best I could by my Leonard," she began. "He was named after my father, he was, and God never breathed life in no better man. He never saw his grandson. If'n he had, maybe Leonard would have…" She was unable to go on.

Tibbs wanted very much to get up and go, leaving the poor woman to her bitter misery, but he knew that he could not do that. When he sensed that the moment was right, he did what he could. "All of Leonard's troubles are over now, Mrs. Tompkins. He will never have to spend another day in jail or face any other problems. Everything has been forgiven." He hoped that somehow that might be true.

"He's in the hands of Lord Jesus now," the woman said. As that thought fixed itself in her mind, she found the beginning of comfort. "His sins been forgiven by the Lamb of God."

"I hope He will do as much for me," Virgil said.

The mother of the dead youth looked at him and slowly nodded. "I knowed you was a good Christian man the way you came to my door and the way you seated yourself. I want you to know my Leonard was born good and would have stayed good if'n he hadn't fallen in with the wrong people. They led him astray. God's my witness, I did my best to teach him right from wrong."

This time Virgil could speak with complete conviction. "He was very lucky to have you for his mother," he said.

"Thank you, sir, thank you." She used the fresh handkerchief once more and then began to say what she felt she must. "He told me that he didn't, but I know that Leonard went and robbed that store in Pasadena, because he stayed out all that night and I didn't know where he was. When he came home finally, the police they was waiting for him. The man who came here was nice. He was a sergeant and he asked if there was anything I needed. My Leonard, he swore terrible; words no young man should ever know or say. He swore he wasn't gonna go back to jail nohow, but then they took him away and I knew from the way he acted that he done wrong again. And he hadn't hardly been home three weeks from the last time."

"You mean, Mrs. Tompkins, the last time that he was in jail?"

"Yes, in jail. With all them murderers and the kind of men that do things to little children."

Tibbs took out his notebook and held a gold Cross pen in his hand. "Mrs. Tompkins, I'm the officer assigned to track down and arrest the man—or men—who did what they did to Leonard. I want to ask your help. Tell me, did he have any enemies? Were there any people who threatened him?"

The large, dark-brown eyes of the bereaved woman stared at him. "I might as well say it," she began, "my boy was a robber, a common thief and a robber. I know, because I found things in his room that didn't belong to him. Things

I know he stole. When he did that to people, he made them enemies, didn't he?"

"Perhaps in most cases they didn't know who he was. Were there any people who knew him by name and who were against him?"

"I can't think of none."

"Do you know if he borrowed money from anyone— especially anyone who might take severe measures to get it back?"

The poor woman shook her head. "He never told we nothin' like that. I always tried to do the best I could for him, even though we're on welfare."

"Your husband…?"

Again she shook her head. "He went away. Almost ten years now. I don't know when he'll be back. I'm afraid for him. He's a painter, but he had trouble finding work."

Tibbs took out a small case and laid a card on the table. "There is my name and telephone number, Mrs. Tompkins," he said. "When you're feeling better, please call me and let me know. I want to talk to you about some of Leonard's friends, but I don't think now is the time."

As he got up she heaved herself to her feet. "Like I said," she told him, "you're a good man in the sight of God." She began to cry again. She was standing in front of the doorway and Tibbs was unable to leave.

"So was the sergeant," she went on finally. "And the others. They was good too. My Leonard hated cops, but he brought the evil onto himself."

When Virgil went back to his car, he was careful not to walk on the thin and discouraged grass.

As he drove toward the freeway, he thought once more of the rope he had seen and a chill settled over him. He knew enough already to be aware that he probably faced a long and difficult investigation. Also, he was almost sure that there would be more violent deaths. For if he was right, the lid of Pandora's box had been flung wide open.

7

Whenever he was involved in a difficult case, or a combination of them, Virgil Tibbs liked to retreat to the privacy of his apartment, where he could rest, listen to the music that he liked best, and think dispassionately about the things he had to do. He sometimes ate in restaurants when he felt the need for an especially good meal; otherwise he fixed his own food, choosing from a strictly limited menu of items that were easy to prepare and required little cleaning up afterward. He knew that there were better ways to live, but he was perhaps a little too aware of the strain that police work almost invariably puts on marriage. The one girl who had attracted his considerable interest in recent years was an heiress and he had hesitated to press forward very fast.

He didn't want to look like, or to be thought, a fortune hunter. He had fought so hard and so long to win himself a place of self-respect, he was probably overcautious to his own detriment. He knew it, but he couldn't help himself.

When he had finished his day's work, he was acutely sensitive to the fact that another aspect of it was about to begin. He wanted to go home, sit down with a cold beer, admire his Holt-Rymers, and listen to Debussy. Instead, he was compelled to face the fact that for the time being he had no home: He would have to go and accommodate himself to another man's family, where there wouldn't be a moment of privacy until he could at last shut the door of the room that had been assigned to him. And he had no idea when it all would end.

He drove to his temporary home in the hills, parked his car in the driveway, and walked up to the front door. It was then that he realized that he had no key and that someone had slipped somewhere. He would have to be seen ringing the bell of what was presumably his own home.

He was within ten feet of the door when it opened and Miriam Motamboru welcomed him with a smile. For just a moment she rested her hands on his shoulders, in the event that anyone was looking, and then ushered him inside. "Did you have a hard day?" she asked.

"Yes," Virgil answered, "and it's going to get worse. The case, I mean," he added quickly.

Miriam went out and returned with a bottle of Peter Heering in one hand and, in the other, a glass with ice cubes. She poured a drink and handed it to him. He took it and looked at her. "You've been well briefed," he said. "Most people don't think of this as a before-dinner drink, but I like it very much."

"Then I'll have some with you," she said. "I'm not sure that my husband would approve, but I shall take the risk."

"As your temporary husband, if the term applies," Tibbs said, "I not only grant my permission, I offer my encouragement."

Miriam went out and returned with another glass. "May I sit by you?" she asked.

"I would be honored," Tibbs answered.

She came and sat by him, but not very close; the foot or two of space between them epitomizing the invisible barrier that would always be there. "Where are the children?" he asked.

"Upstairs," she answered. "They have a television program they want to see and it's all very new to them, of course. I encourage it because it will help them with their English."

"I'm not a very good father," Tibbs said. "I don't know their names."

Miriam smiled charmingly, and he felt a flash of warning, not for fear of her but of himself. "Your daughter's name is Annette," she told him. "And your son is Pierre. He is named for a very close friend of my husband's."

"Have you cautioned them about . . . their new role?"

"Yes," she answered. "Very carefully. I realize that you are not a father as yet, but I can tell you that children are far more understanding and resourceful than you might ever imagine. I explained to them why you are here and they understood perfectly. They will also obey you just as though you were their own father. After you are no longer required to be their father, I hope that you will consent to be their uncle."

Before Virgil could respond to that, she got up, walked over to his stereo, and put on a record. "I know that you like Ravel," she said. "How about *Valses nobles et sentimentales?*" She smiled pleasantly, making things as agreeable for him as she could. He noted at once how smoothly and easily she pronounced the French title.

There were sounds from the staircase and the two children came into the room. They stopped when they were a few feet away and young Pierre obviously did as he had been instructed. He approached Tibbs and gravely held out his hand. "Good evening, sir," he said.

Tibbs leaned forward and accepted the hand. "I'm glad to see you," he said.

The little girl was bolder; she climbed up beside him and planted a kiss on his cheek. In response, he picked her up and put her on his knee. "Thank you, Annette," he said. "I liked that very much."

"You're going to be a nice daddy," she answered. She fought to form the words in a language strange to her and he realized immediately that she had been rehearsed. He set her down carefully and turned to Miriam. "They're beautiful children," he told her. "I hope someday that I may meet the President and congratulate him."

Miriam got to her feet and dazzled him with a smile, but bright as it was, there was restraint in it also. "I'll look after dinner," she said. "Do you like French cooking?"

"With a few exceptions," he confessed.

"Such as?"

"Not until I know what you are serving first."

She smiled again. "Don't worry, Virgil, I know better than to cook *tripes à la mode de Caen* for an American. It is an acquired taste. We are having *gigot d'agneau à la provençale*, which is leg of lamb."

"I'm overwhelmed," Tibbs said.

"Wait until you've tasted it first. Also, I chose the wine; I hope you will approve."

"I must confess that I'm not much of a wine drinker."

She looked at him, an eyebrow raised. "But, of course, you were probably raised on the purely local product."

"When I was a boy," Virgil told her, "we were poor Negroes in the Deep South. Sometimes the food we ate was what was left over after all the palatable cuts had been sold to white customers. We didn't dine—we survived."

That shook Miriam up and for a few seconds she did not know what to say. Then she took the only tack she could. "I was much more fortunate. Almost from the beginning I was raised to become a woman of quality; in that environment my color meant very little. My people, you see, were wealthy and they arranged the best possible education for me." She stopped and looked at him, asking his understanding. "I know now that yours was the much greater achievement. Dinner will be ready in about ten minutes."

Virgil went to his room, put on a fresh Don Loper shirt, and prepared himself for his first experience as the head of a family at the table. When he came down, the children were standing by their chairs, waiting for him to be seated first. "Don't wait for me," Miriam said. "Go right ahead with the soup. I have a few more things to do."

Despite that, the children waited patiently until their mother had taken her place at the table opposite Tibbs. Then the meal began in an atmosphere of constrained formality. Fortunately the mood did not last long. Before the soup was half gone, Pierre leaned forward and asked, "Are you really a detective?"

"Yes, I am," Tibbs said.

"And do you catch murderers?"

"I'm trying to catch one now." He noted that despite his accent, the little boy had already acquired a fair understanding of English. He was not yet fluent, but he was able to think out what he wanted to say and then put it into words. At eight years of age that was a major achievement. It was quite some family that had been given to him; for a brief moment he wondered if he would be able to live up to them.

But he soon stopped worrying because the food was superb and he was expected to converse for the children's benefit. Before the meal was half over, he began to enjoy his role: He answered questions about the police department and gave some advice about living in the United States. He knew that the children wouldn't be going out except under careful supervision, but they still should be taught.

After the meal was over, he offered to help in the kitchen but was refused. "I have a dishwasher and everything I need," Miriam told him. "Just go and do whatever you like to do most evenings."

That effectively burst the tiny bubble of fantasy that had been building in him; he no longer pretended that he was indeed the head of this unique family. He watched one of the few television programs about policemen that he approved of and then went up early to his room. Most of his books were there and he chose one in the hope that he would lose himself in its pages.

Miss Griswold, the librarian, called him in the morning. Since the library was close by, he walked over to see what the reference specialist had been able to uncover for him.

As always, she was pleasant and informative. "There is a great deal of material on capital punishment," she began. "Most of it is devoted to arguing for and against it as a means of justice. I didn't think that you wanted any of that."

"Right," Tibbs agreed.

"There are also a number of books on ancient torture methods that are pretty terrible. However, there is some material on hanging in them. I have two here that may help you. Now, as to modern-day hangings, there isn't anything I could find that describes how it should be done— no manual for executioners."

"I would hardly expect anything like that to exist," Tibbs said.

"You would be surprised at some of the things in print, Mr. Tibbs. However, I did run down two items for you that may be helpful. The first: the memoirs of Albert Pierrepont, the famous British executioner. The copyright is 1974 and it does contain a great deal of technical information about execution by hanging, though not in a grim way. I'm sure the author knows his subject."

"I'm certain of that, Miss Griswold."

"Then there is another book that might help you. It's a novel by James McClure called *The Sunday Hangman*. He's quite a famous writer about South Africa. There's a lot about hanging in that book too."

Tibbs smiled a little grimly. "As always, Miss Griswold, you're the completely resourceful librarian. I'm sorry that I had to bring you such a morbid topic."

"Then maybe you'll do me a favor." The librarian looked at him with studied innocence.

"Did you get a ticket?" Tibbs asked.

"No, nothing like that. I just want to ask you a question."

"Then go ahead."

"You know, I read all the books about you; they're quite popular here. Did you actually work on a murder case in a nudist colony?"

Tibbs reminded himself to be patient. "Not a colony, Miss Griswold, a resort. Yes, I did."

"And was there a young woman called Linda who lived there?"

"Yes, she gave me her picture." He realized at once that that was probably the understatement of his career.

Without saying another word the librarian reached over to one side of her desk and handed him four books. As he picked them up, she found her voice. "Return them anytime," she said. "Whenever you're through."

*　　　*　　　*

Willis Raymond was hiding out in his apartment, and for that Tibbs couldn't blame him. A heavy dressing covered the top of his head, his nose displayed visible stitches, and his lower jaw was concealed behind a mass of tape and gauze. He had to be in more or less continuous pain and he didn't even have the comfort of knowing that he was healing because a good deal of dental restorative work would have to be done and that would be another ordeal. Even with modern anesthesia it would still be a long and painful process.

As he came in, Virgil took time to look around the fairly large furnished room. It wasn't much to come back to after a day's work. It was possible that the clerk chose to live simply so that he could save some money. It seemed at times as if most of humanity was enduring the present largely because it held out hopes for the Future: something a little better, some extra money to spend, a son or daughter in cap and gown graduating from college.

Despite his injuries, Raymond could talk fairly well through his bruised lips. He sat in the only comfortable chair and waited while Tibbs took one of the two chairs that were pulled up to a plain round table. "I gave my whole story to the cops—at the hospital," the clerk said. "I was full of dope then and it didn't hurt so much."

Despite that, Tibbs sensed that he was willing to be drawn out, probably for the sake of someone to talk to. That and the elementary human need for some form of recognition.

"I know, Mr. Raymond," Virgil answered. "I've read the reports very carefully. I want to compliment you on being so clearheaded at a time when you must have been in severe pain."

"I'm not exactly comfortable right now," Raymond said.

"Believe me, I understand that," Tibbs told him. "And I appreciate what it means for you to talk to me."

That hit exactly the right note. "I want to do all that I can to help," the clerk responded, accepting the credit that he knew was his due.

51

"Let me save you some trouble," Virgil said. "I understand that two young black men came into your store shortly before closing time. You sensed immediately that they might be planning a holdup, so you very wisely tripped the alarm."

"No, I moved where I could trip it and waited. As soon as one of the nig . . . punks pulled out a gun and yelled 'Freeze!'—*then* I tripped it."

Tibbs nodded his approval. "I understand that about eighty per cent of the customers who shop in your store are black."

"That's right." Raymond was anxious to recover from his blunder. "And most of 'em are good people. They come in, they get what they want, they pay, and they never give me any trouble. Like that Mrs. Meecker: I know she helped you draw the picture of the asshole who did this to me."

"More than that," Tibbs added, "she's willing to testify. So is Mrs. Carmichael, the white lady who also helped with the picture."

"They're all right," Raymond said.

Tibbs purposely became a bit more formal. "I understand, sir, that according to your statement you had never seen either of the bandits before they came into your store."

"That's right. The paper said they were from Los Angeles."

"The paper was right. Now I want to ask you if being unable to work for the time being is causing you any hardship."

Raymond shifted in his chair, the heavy bandages on his head making him look a little like the invisible man. "It's nice of you to ask that. No, I'm all right. Mr. Goldfarb, who owns the store, told me that he'll keep my salary going until I can go back to work. And he's going to transfer me to another of his stores where there's less risk. As assistant manager." He added the last phrase with a touch of pride; the Future had come just a little closer.

"And your medical bills?"

"The store has insurance. And this is one claim they're

not going to be able to wiggle out of paying. You know how they are."

Tibbs went on to another topic. "Since the robbery, has anyone approached you concerning your testimony?"

"The newspaper people; they been here."

"What I meant was: Has anyone tried to get you to back down from identifying the suspects? I'll keep your answer strictly confidential."

"No."

"Has anyone approached you with the idea of getting revenge for what you have had to suffer?"

"No. One guy called me and said that he could get me a good deal on having my teeth fixed."

"Did he identify himself?"

"He gave me his name, but I don't remember it now."

"Did he mention the doctor he had in mind?"

"Some guy in Los Angeles, that's all I remember. I didn't pay much attention to it. A lot of lawyers wrote me saying that a friend of mine had asked them to send me their card and for me to let them know if they could be of any help. I haven't got that many friends."

"Have you engaged a lawyer on your own?"

"No, I don't want one. One guy I know, he had a little auto accident and he hired a lawyer. By the time he had paid him off, he didn't have enough left to get his car fixed."

Tibbs rose to go. "Thank you for your time," he said. "I know how you must feel, and you have my sympathy."

He paused and thought for a moment before he said anything more. Then he decided to add what he had in mind. "You have one comfort, anyway. The man who hit you is dead, so he'll never do it again—to you or anyone else."

Raymond reacted to that. "The guy who got hung wasn't the asshole who hit me. It was the other one."

8

For the next three days Tibbs was in court. He sat and waited on the hard seats, ready to be called to the stand, while the legal maneuvering went on and on. Across from him a traffic officer in full gear waited from early morning until close to four in the afternoon to give evidence in another case. The judge postponed it.

That was the first day. On the second day the defense attorney quibbled endlessly, trying to get his guilty client off on some technicality. Other witnesses, too, were kept waiting. When the session finally ended, Tibbs went back to his temporary home with a strong sense of frustration gnawing at him. Miriam had prepared another excellent dinner, but the good food did little to make him feel any better.

After the children had been put to bed, she came and sat with him, offering companionship without intimacy. "Tell me about it, Virgil," she suggested.

He shook his head. "I don't want to, Miriam. Too many police marriages go on the rocks because what goes on in the streets is brought home." He realized at once what he had said and tried to think of a graceful way out, but Miriam spared him the trouble.

"It's a very unusual thing," she said. "I'm happily married to a man who is thousands of miles away—and being looked after by another. But while we are both in this difficult position, I'm glad that you feel the way you do about us. That you have accepted us so fully." She stopped for a moment and then pitched her voice a little lower. "I know, of course, that you had no real choice and, above all, we don't want to be an undue burden on you."

When she stopped speaking it was very hard for Virgil to sit perfectly still and resist putting his arm around her by way of reassurance. He was embarrassingly aware of her femininity and he could not block it out of his mind.

"I don't know how long this will last," he said, choosing his words carefully, "but you and the children will never be a burden." He forced himself to smile. "Not the way that you mean. And I hope to meet your husband someday."

"Of course you will," she answered. "We will want you for a close friend of the family."

There was something behind that remark he could not decipher. Usually he was very good at discovering hidden meanings in the words people spoke, but in Miriam's case his ability seemed to desert him. He thought of going up to his room, but it was still very early in the evening.

He had an idea that appealed to him and he acted on it. "I have a suggestion," he said. "Please tell me if you like it or not."

"Go ahead," she invited.

"Except for going to the market, you're housebound here all day. I know how tight security is, but if you did go out, there's almost no chance of your being recognized—except in certain circumstances. And those could be avoided."

She reached out and laid her fingers gently on top of his. "Thank you for offering to escort me. If the people who are responsible for me approve, I'd like to go very much."

"Bob Nakamura could baby-sit," Virgil said. "You understand that I'm not trying to force myself on you."

She reassured him with a small pressure from her fingers.

"And perhaps I could take Pierre to a baseball game."

"I'm sure he'd like that," she answered quickly. "He is already watching all the games he can on television. His father has always encouraged an interest in sports. Not the cruel ones, like bullfighting, but good athletic competition."

"Then I'll take him," Tibbs said. "And if the people you spoke of approve, I'd like to take the children to the zoo."

"Does that include me?" Miriam asked.

"Yes, if you don't mind the walking."

She smiled, teasing him just a little. "You've never seen Bakara. If you had, you wouldn't worry about that. Incidentally, I ride a horse quite well."

At that he shook his head. "I can't ride," he admitted. "And if you were to get involved with the people who do, there might be an increased chance of your being recognized."

She pursed her lips slightly. "I don't think that too likely. But if you think it better not . . . "

"I do," Tibbs said. "You know what precautions have been taken up to now. Even totally reliable top members of our department don't know that you're here, or that I'm posing as your husband. In the normal crowd at the zoo the odds against your being recognized are too remote to worry about. On a horse you would be a lot more conspicuous."

Miriam nodded. "I see your point," she conceded. "Because I'm African, I would be noticed, perhaps. Someone might talk."

"Yes," Tibbs agreed. "And there's something else. I don't want to alarm you, but your absence at home must have been noticed by now. I've been told that your husband has some very resourceful enemies. I have to assume that they're actively looking for you."

"They probably are," Miriam said.

"You know that even highly classified information is sometimes compromised. The CIA has been betrayed in the past by some of its own people. Somewhere between Bakara and here something could have leaked. About a young woman who rides horses exceptionally well."

Miriam turned toward him more, an action that accidentally brought them a little closer together. "Virgil," she said, looking him full in the face, "I want you to know that I have great confidence in you—and trust. If I can't be with my husband, then I don't know anyone else I'd rather

56

have looking after me. You tell us what to do and we'll follow your instructions exactly."

There was a look of genuine concern on Tibbs's features, but he banished it and smiled at her. "We'll manage," he said. "You keep up the great cooking, that's your part. I'll do my very best for you and the children."

Emily Myerson was walking alone down the street. It did not disturb her that it was almost eleven at night and that the lighting was not very good. She had thoroughly enjoyed the movie and the euphoria it had induced was still with her. It even convinced her a little that she was an attractive young woman despite the fact that she was forty pounds overweight, that she had acne, and that her hair was no real help to her at all.

She had been told that she was a hopeless case, but she was not yet ready to accept that status. It was Saturday night and practically every girl in town was out on a date, but Emily did not let that defeat her. She clung to her rationalization that the right man would find her; until he did, she was more than happy to wait.

It also helped when she reminded herself that she was a "good" girl: she had preserved her virginity even though she knew that almost all the more popular girls were having active sex lives. They often talked about it, discussing in detail the thrills they enjoyed and the attention they received. Emily had had very little temptation to emulate them; sexual invitations, like more conventional ones, were seldom pressed on her. She walked on, still thinking about the fantasy world into which she had been admitted for an hour and a half in return for the admission price.

When the old Chevrolet zoomed past her, she did not particularly notice it, not even when it quite suddenly slowed up and pulled to the curb a hundred and fifty feet ahead of her. She was still walking, not in Pasadena, but on the yellow brick road of that other world she was so reluctant to surrender. She was vaguely aware when all four doors of the car opened and four young men got out. Obviously they had friends in the neighborhood.

They stood around the car, talking to themselves until she was almost abreast of them; then she was abruptly jerked out of the remaining fragments of her reverie when they sauntered over and intercepted her. She realized in a flash that one was behind her, two others were on either side, and the fourth was standing on the sidewalk directly in front of her. There was no way she could pass him quietly by.

She knew that she was going to have to talk to them and she did not know what she was going to say. She had never acquired the knack of casual greetings and was afraid that she would give offense. She was far more sensitive than most people knew and she could not bear to make anyone feel uncomfortable or unhappy.

She decided to smile at the man in front of her in a pleasant way and keep on walking. Her resolution made, she took a few more steps and acknowledged the young man's presence. As she moved forward, the two others who were stationed at her side kept pace.

The one she had smiled at stepped directly in front of her and forced her to stop. As he did so, the others drew closer.

"You don't wanna be out alone like this," the man in front said. "It ain't safe."

"Oh I'll be all right," Emily answered. "I don't have far to go. But thank you." She passed immediate judgment on her own words and decided that she had done well.

"You better ride with us," the young man said. "We'll take you home."

"No, please, don't bother." She was aware then, as he came closer, of a strong body odor that told of clothes too long unwashed and bad personal hygiene. It came at her in a wave and she tried not to show how it was affecting her.

"What's 'sa matta?" she was asked. "You afraid of us 'cause we're black?"

"Of course not," she answered with some indignation. She had taken pride for some time in the fact that she was without prejudice. When someone jokingly asked her if she

58

would allow a black student to escort her to a party, she answered that if he were a gentleman she would be pleased to accept. Now the reality confronted her and she knew with almost piercing awareness that these were not the same kind of well-bred young black people she had met. They were coming in closer and fresh odors began to assail her, including a sickly sweet one she could not identify.

"That's it, guys," the one in front of her said. "She don' wanna have nothin' to do wit' us, cause we's black."

"That's ridiculous!" she countered, trying to make it sound convincing; partly to convince them, partly to re-enforce her own belief. Nothing like this had ever happened to her before.

The one in front of her put his right hand on her shoulder and his fingers took a tight enough grip to let her know that he meant business. "You say you ain't 'fraid of us 'cause we're black. Now you prove it. You get in, we know you're O.K. We'll take you right home." He looked up at the others. "That right, men?"

The three others answered, agreeing. Emily was not sure what they had said, but she heard "Right on, Jerry" and "That's right, man," and from those words she rebuilt a shattered facsimile of hope. There was no reason why they would all lie to her; that had to be the truth. She tried desperately to convince herself of it.

"Come on, we're wastin' time," the leader said, and with his hand still on her shoulder he turned her toward the car.

Home was not far away; she should be there within two minutes. They just wanted her to prove that a white girl would ride with them; if it was anything else, they would have gone for one of the pretty ones—there were so many around.

When the leader held open the back door, she climbed inside. She hoped that a police car might come by and stop to investigate, but the street remained deserted. Perhaps since Proposition 13 there were fewer police on the streets—she was not sure. The opposite car door opened and she found herself in the middle. The odor became much more unpleasant.

She had a sudden intense desire to flee, but she was already jammed so tightly she could hardly move at all. She knew that she would never be able to get either door open, much less regain her freedom. The only chance she had was to hope and pray that they did intend to take her home.

The leader, who was sitting to her right, asked, "Where you live now?" and her spirits soared. She quickly gave him the address. As the car started, she wondered if she was expected to invite them in: They might take offense if she didn't make some gesture.

"We'll take you home now," the leader said. "We'll ride around a little first, get acquainted, then we'll go right to your place."

"I'd like to go there right now, if you don't mind," Emily said. She tried to make her voice sound pleasant, as though she were speaking to newfound friends.

"First we'll ride around. Then, like I said, we'll drop you off. Right at your door. Right, men?"

A chorus of three added its solemn agreement.

The car headed north, toward the towering mountain that almost overshadowed the city. The driver seemed to know the way; he was not even pretending to be casual.

In ten minutes they were high enough for the lights of Pasadena to spread below them in a fine panorama. Then the pavement suddenly ended and the car bumped onto a dirt road, one that was obviously very little traveled.

Emily's throat was parched as she tried to realize that the sort of thing she had heard about, and that always happened to other people, might be happening to her. She was terrified; in her frantic brain the most that she dared hope for was that somehow she would escape unscathed.

The car stopped. Emily was determined to fight for her life, but even in her frenzy she knew that there was no possible hope: She could never overcome four strong young men. She began to feel light-headed and then something in her brain seemed to snap.

*   *   *

It was 1:57 A.M. when the call came in to the Pasadena police switchboard. Police clerk Kathleen Pittaway took the call and wrote rapidly on the form in front of her. The man's voice, though cultivated and restrained, was clearly agitated.

"I don't want to create a problem," the caller said. "But as I said, our daughter was due home about eleven, almost three hours ago. We've called all her friends and no one has seen her. I looked up and down the streets myself and drove along Colorado Boulevard, but I couldn't find a trace of her."

"May I have her description, please," Kathleen asked. She took down the data quickly and efficiently. As soon as the caller hung up, she went at once to the duty sergeant.

Sergeant Ben Hetherington read the cryptic facts and went in immediately to see the watch commander.

"We've got another girl missing," he said, "and from the looks of it I don't like it at all."

The watch commander put out the call and sent four special units to check the city's known isolated areas.

Sergeant Terry Blumenthal and his partner found her twenty-three minutes later. They radioed at once for paramedics and then called, in code fashion, to notify the watch commander.

"We have a two sixty-one in S-4 condition," he reported. "Request full backup for two o seven suspected. Description matches." He added this in the hope that there was no way that the parents of the victim at his feet could be listening to police frequency two, the one that was normally reserved for special uses.

The watch commander heard the message on the monitor in his office and clenched his teeth as he thought of his own eighteen-year-old daughter. Then he dialed the confidential emergency number he had been given to reach Virgil Tibbs.

9

Virgil Tibbs took the call on the special line that had been installed at his bedside. The number was highly restricted so that it would be free as much as possible. An extension rang in the living room, but the phone there was kept carefully out of sight and even the children did not know that it existed.

"Yes?" he asked as soon as he was awake.

"Watch commander, Virgil. Sorry to disturb you, but we've got a bad one: rape with serious bodily harm. The victim is at Huntington, still incoherent. It looks like a gang attack."

"Who's at Huntington now?"

"Ben Hetherington."

"I'll make it as fast as I can."

That was a slight change in his normal procedure. The Huntington Memorial Hospital was only a short distance from his regular apartment and he would have given an ETA of less than fifteen minutes. Since he was then on the east side of the city, he avoided giving his estimated time of arrival in specific figures.

He turned on his bedside lamp and dialed Chief Mc-Gowan's number from memory. As soon as he had an answer, he explained, "I've just been called in for a possible gang two sixty-one with serious bodily injury. I'll be leaving here shortly; I don't know for how long."

McGowan understood at once; in fact, the last sentence was unnecessary. "I'll take care of it," he said.

That duty discharged, Virgil dressed as quickly and as quietly as he could. Usually he went to work in sports clothes, but this time he chose a plain dark suit and a somber tie, something better suited to the hour and the situation that faced him. There would probably be family members to interview and they would expect him to appear as businesslike as possible.

He opened the door of his room and was startled to find Miriam there in a dressing gown. She had tied it loosely around her waist, but it did not conceal the separation between her breasts. "Virgil, what is it?" she asked. Her voice was tense and fearful.

"I've been called out," he told her. "A crime—rape. Nothing to do with you or the children."

"Can I fix you something? Some hot chocolate?" She already knew that he liked it.

"No time, I'm afraid," he answered. "I've got to leave right now. I don't know when I'll be back, but I called the chief and he knows. You'll be protected."

"Will you be in any danger?"

"I don't think so, Miriam. Go back to bed and don't worry."

She ignored his instructions. As he ran down the stairs toward the front door, she followed close behind, as agile on her feet as he was on his. When he opened the door, she was there beside him to see him off.

He turned once again to tell her to go back. Her eyes opened slightly wider and she spoke to him in an undertone of urgency. "Kiss me, kiss me quickly." She held out her arms.

For a fraction of a second he hesitated, thinking that she was emotionally upset. Then his brain functioned and he understood. He took her into his arms and kissed her as any departing husband would do under the same circumstances. He turned and saw a car parked less than a hundred feet up the cul-de-sac with a man visible in it. It was light tan and he knew at once that it was one of his own department's unmarked units.

He quickly got into his own vehicle and started backing

out of the garage before the door mechanism had completed its cycle. He turned and drove away, ignoring the presence of the waiting car and the man in it. He turned onto the street that led downhill, opened the glove compartment door, and clicked on the police radio that was concealed there. He requested a switch to channel two, which bypassed all of the routine radio traffic, and asked, "Have we a code five going near the chief's house?"

"Negative."

That shook him. He was certain that he had recognized a departmental vehicle.

"Twenty-three Henry four."

That was his call and he answered. "Twenty-three Henry four—by."

"Twenty-three Henry four, ten twenty-two."

That was all he needed to hear; for some reason he was to disregard the information he had been given. He signed off and clipped the microphone back where it belonged. After that he concentrated entirely on his driving until he pulled into one of the reserved parking spots at Huntington Memorial Hospital and placed his card on the instrument deck where it could be seen from the outside. Then he locked up and went into the emergency entrance.

Ben Hetherington met him there; the stocky, solidly built sergeant had worked homicide himself for years and was one of the department's experts. "You're just in time," he said. "The victim is beginning to come round and she may be able to talk to us."

"How old is she?"

"Nineteen."

"Parents here?"

"Father; he's climbing the walls. He was offered a sedative and refused."

"I don't blame him."

Together with Hetherington he went to the nurses' station outside the emergency room. "What's the latest?" he asked.

"I think you can go in, Mr. Tibbs, but please be careful."

"Depend on it," he responded.

64

He walked a few steps to the emergency room door and pushed it open just enough to see inside. A nurse came up quickly to chase him away, but when she opened the door he was holding his badge for her to see.

"Are you the investigator?" she asked.

"Yes, one of them."

"All right, then, but keep away from her until the doctor tells you differently."

Virgil slipped inside and carefully took up a position against the wall where he could see and hear everything that was going on without interfering. When the doctor glanced toward him he displayed his badge once more; otherwise he remained perfectly still.

He studied the victim who lay on the table. He knew at once that she had been genuinely assaulted and that she had fought to defend herself. Her face was badly scratched and there was blood visible on the small pile of her clothing that had been put on a stool. She was covered with a sheet that did not conceal the ample size of her body. Her glasses had been removed, but her hair, even in disarray, made it clear that she had not competed as a beauty. It was cut short and showed no signs of curling or shaping.

The doctor checked the pupils of her eyes with an ophthalmoscope and then looked up. "You're Tibbs, aren't you?" he asked.

"Yes."

"You're going to handle this case?"

"I've been assigned."

"All right, I'll give it to you straight. All the medical evidence points to a gang rape. In my opinion she was a *virgin intacta* when she was assaulted. There's ample medical evidence to prove that she resisted, probably to the limit of her ability."

"I did." The barely audible words came from the patient, who had hardly moved her lips.

The doctor immediately gave her his full attention. "This is the police detective in charge. Tell me your age again."

"Nineteen."

"Do I have your permission to discuss all necessary medical details with him?"

"Yes." The tightness in her voice betrayed the state of her mind.

Tibbs walked over to the table where she was lying and allowed her to look at him while he studied her. He saw her eyes widen when she realized that he was a Negro; from that fact he made an immediate deduction.

"I'm Virgil Tibbs of the Pasadena Police Department," he said. "I specialize in serious crimes against persons: things like murder, felonious assault, and rape. Do you understand me?"

"Yes." Her eyes were wide open and she trembled as if on the verge of shock.

"What's your first name?"

"Emily."

"Emily, were you attacked by several men?"

"Yes."

"How many?"

"Four."

"What kind of men?"

"Young."

"Younger or older than you?"

The patient did not speak for several seconds; then she said, "Older."

"Were they black?"

"Yes."

"All four?"

"Yes."

"Did you know them?"

"No."

"Had you ever seen them before?"

"No."

"Did you go with them willingly?"

That was a mistake. Abruptly the patient raised her arms and covered her face with her hands. He saw her broken nails and when he looked very closely, he saw that there were bits of blood and skin trapped under them. That was vital evidence and would have to be preserved with the greatest care.

He remained quiet and waited, letting her recover whatever bit of composure she had left. Finally she spoke between her fingers. "No."

"That's enough for now," Tibbs said. "Later, when you feel better, I want to ask you about their car. That will help a great deal—anything you can tell me."

Slowly Emily drew her hands down and let him see the tears that were flowing from her eyes. She turned her head a little toward him and her lips quivered as she tried once more to speak. "I want to die," she said.

Tibbs took a step forward and, against all good judgment, took one of her hands into his. He held it for a moment, letting her feel his presence. After that he knew she was not locked into a world of prejudice, that eventually she would accept and help him.

"You've just had a terrible experience," he told her. "But you are in good hands now. Physically you should be all right in a few days. The shock is going to last longer, but it will go away, too, if you let it. We all get hurt and we heal. You will too."

He stopped, hoping he had not been too maudlin. Because the wretchedly abused girl was still close to the edge, he had kept his words very simple, but as convincing as he could make them.

It was quiet. He put her hand down very gently and gave it a very slight, reassuring pat to let her know that he was concerned.

He was turning away when she spoke again. "The car."

He was listening intently. "Yes?"

"The license. I know part . . ."

"Please tell me!"

"It was V . . . R . . . G . . . nine something."

If she was right, that would narrow the field down to a hundred possible vehicles.

"New or old?" he asked, very gently.

"Old."

"One last question: Can you tell me the make or the color?"

Emily moved her lips without speaking. The doctor drew closer to the table and Tibbs knew that he could not stay any longer. He stepped back a pace or two to show that he understood. The doctor put his hand on her forehead and spoke with an equally quiet voice. "I saw you inspecting her hands. I'll have the scrapings from under her nails kept for evidence. I'll seal them in an envelope and sign and date it. And I'll give you the results of the smears and semen tests."

"Thank you."

Tibbs turned to go when the voice of the victim was suddenly heard in the emergency room. "V-R-G," she cried out with pathetic weakness. "V-R-G . . . for virgin."

10

When Virgil Tibbs walked into his second-floor office the following morning, Bob Nakamura greeted him silently by pointing toward the ceiling. "The Man," he said.

"Now?"

"Right now."

Virgil went back to the elevator and took it up to the fourth-floor executive suite. When he appeared at the chief's office, Mrs. Stone, McGowan's confidential secretary, gave him a smile. "Go right in, Virgil," she said. "He's expecting you."

"Thank you." He walked into the chief's office and closed the door. McGowan was behind his desk, but he got up and walked over to the near corner of the office where there were comfortable chairs.

"Sit down, Virgil," he said. "When I got that call from you last night, I considered it possible that it might have been a device to get you out of the way."

"The same thought crossed my mind," Tibbs said. "Which is why I woke you up."

McGowan sat down. "So I called our friends who set up your present assignment. They covered very quickly."

"Using one of our cars?"

"One just like ours." He leaned forward a little. "A very close watch is being kept on that house and the family that's in it. There's at least one very powerful organization that's sworn to overthrow Motamboru by any means."

"I know that, sir. Mrs. Motamboru is very uptight about

69

it. She's doing her best to be a good hostess and mother, but the strain on her must be terrible. I can see it."

McGowan shifted his position a little. "Which brings up something else, Virgil. You were cautioned that no matter what the circumstances, Mrs. Motamboru had to be totally hands off. I thought I made that clear."

"You did." Tibbs looked at him squarely and without emotion. "When I came in last night, she heard my phone ring and got up. When I came out of my room, she was waiting for me to find out what was wrong. She was very concerned."

"Of course."

"I told her that I had been called in on a police matter that didn't concern her or the children so as to put her mind at ease. As I was leaving, she came to the door with me. When I turned to tell her to go back inside, she spotted the car parked a short distance away with someone in it."

He stopped, but the chief did not interrupt him.

"She literally grasped the whole thing in a flash and quietly and urgently told me to kiss her. I admit that for a second I didn't get it—I thought she was being overemotional. Then I understood and kissed her as a departing husband should. I gathered that someone was watching, but I had no idea who."

McGowan tapped his fingernails on the edge of the chair. "That makes sense; I'm glad you explained it. Obviously that lady can think for herself. She must be stimulating company."

"She certainly is. She can talk on almost any topic. She's fluent in several languages and has a remarkable grasp of international politics. Also, she is a whale of a cook and knows how to raise her kids."

The chief looked thoughtful. "Virgil, it can't always be too easy for you under the circumstances."

"It isn't that bad," Tibbs answered. "I know what my responsibility is and I'm careful not to forget it. Miriam is devoted to her husband—that's very clear. She's a charming hostess, but it could never go beyond that. We both understand that point fully and respect it."

McGowan was obviously satisfied because he changed the topic. "How about the two sixty-one last night—any leads?"

"The victim gave me a partial on the car license. I worked on it last night and came up with four good possibles, assuming that the victim was right. She was in pretty tough shape and half out of her mind."

McGowan nodded. "Keep after it even if you have to put some other things aside. Ask Dick Smith to assign them to someone else."

"Yes, sir."

Virgil was glad to escape from the office. He had told the absolute truth about the incident McGowan had questioned, but he was acutely aware of what he had not said. He would never confide *that* to anyone, but when he had held Miriam close to him for a moment, and had kissed her even briefly, a fire had coursed through his whole being. He could still feel the gentle pressure of her lips against his, as though they had never been taken away.

The investigation into the death of Leonard Tompkins was rapidly coming to a dead end. A careful check of the area where his body had been found had turned up nothing at all. No one came forward with any information; there weren't even any crank calls to check out. Not a snitch on the street knew anything at all or had heard even the vaguest of rumors. A thorough check into Tompkins' background showed that he had been in constant trouble since he was twelve years old. He had dropped out of school early and had been all but illiterate. He had a history of drug abuse, sexual offenses, burglary, and, later, armed robbery. His mother had continued steadfastly to believe in him. The unofficial police position was that someone had removed an all but worthless member of society from the scene, but that did not alter the fact that it was still murder.

Only one fact seemed clear: no single person could have taken him up onto that balcony and then hanged him. Tompkins was quite muscular and had once taken out a

71

boxer's license. The most reasonable explanation was that he had been unconscious when he had been suspended on the end of the rope, but the coroner's findings showed nothing that might have induced such a state. One possibility was present: He had been a user of deadly PCP ("angel dust") and that drug could send its victims off into a state of euphoria at any time. In such a trance, he could either have been as inert as a corpse or suddenly so violently active that he would have had superhuman strength. There were two cases on file where PCP users had been able to rip steel handcuffs off their wrists. They had done terrible damage to themselves, tearing their flesh and ligaments almost beyond repair, but because of the drug they had felt no pain whatever.

It was possible that one or two persons had come upon Tompkins in a catatonic state and had hanged him. But the big argument against that was the well-prepared rope. Such things do not come to hand by accident.

The homicide team assigned to the field investigation came back empty-handed. The autopsy report contained nothing suggestive. The L.A.P.D. had a good file on the deceased, but it shed no light on who had murdered him. It was, for the time being, an almost total washout. Tibbs regretfully put it on the back burner, waiting for the break that, sooner or later, might come.

Of the four likely suspect cars in the rape case, one was eliminated because the owner-driver had been stopped for running a red light at almost the same time that the attack on Emily Myerson had taken place. It was probably the luckiest ticket of his life, as he was a known sex offender. The other three cars were registered in various parts of the sheriff's jurisdiction; detectives from the Hall of Justice were checking them out.

Virgil broke his silence. "I'm going to the hospital to see the victim," he said.

Bob Nakamura looked up from his own work. "Isn't it policy for female officers to take the victim's statement?"

"Yes, but I'm not going for that. I just want to ask her one question."

"You could have done that last night."

"No, I couldn't. She was in near shock and couldn't have told me one more thing. So I'll try again."

He put on his coat and went downstairs. On the way he stopped at a florist's shop. When he arrived at the hospital, he had a bouquet wrapped in green tissue paper.

Emily was in bed with the back cranked up so that she was in a semi-erect posture. She had been put in a single room at the request of the police department; the hospital usually co-operated in such matters. She had on a plain hospital gown, but she had combed her hair—or someone had done it for her.

Tibbs presented himself quietly, almost as though he had accidentally dropped in. "Good morning, Emily," he said. "You may not remember me, but we met last night."

"I know who you are," she said.

Tibbs walked to her bedside and handed her the bouquet. The girl looked at it, peered inside, and then unwrapped it slowly until she held the roses mixed with baby's breath in her hands. "Watch out for the thorns," he said.

Emily seemed to have retreated momentarily into a fog. "Are these for me?" she asked incredulously.

Tibbs smiled. "Who else?" he asked.

Emily looked at them; then her throat closed and a gentle sob was heard. When she looked up, in embarrassment, her eyes were moist. "The first time," she said. "The first time anyone ever gave me flowers. And I had to get raped to earn them!"

Virgil quietly took her hand. "Last night," he said, "you showed rare courage—and intelligence. You gave me part of a license number. That's my thank-you to you. Please accept my admiration too."

Emily swallowed hard and composed herself. "Thank you," she said. "Maybe one of the nurses can put these in water for me." Emily reached for the bell push pinned to the bedding. When the nurse came in, she already knew what was wanted.

"I'll fix them for you," she offered and went out with the flowers in her hands.

Virgil turned toward his subject. "Emily, to put your mind at rest, I'm not going to ask you for a statement now. Some of our girls from the department will be over to see you later about that."

"I don't care," she said. "I don't care at all." Then she denied her own words by turning her head until her face was half buried in the pillow.

"I do," Tibbs replied. "Actually, if you can answer it, I'd like to ask you just one question. That's all."

"One question?"

"One."

"What is it?"

"I know that four young blacks attacked you. I know that it was savage and brutal, and I don't want to go over any of that now. Here is my question: At any time, did you hear any of them call each other by name? And if they did, can you remember any name at all that was used? I cheated, I asked two questions." Then he waited.

He seemed to relax completely, as though the answer was not of major concern to him at all. His casualness apparently helped to put Emily at ease—or at least to keep her further from the brink of an emotional upset when she had to turn her thoughts back to what had been done to her.

A long, silent minute went by; Tibbs looked out the window and continued to suggest that he was in no hurry at all. The nurse came in quietly with the flowers he had brought, now nicely arranged in a vase. She put the bouquet at Emily's bedside, smiled, and withdrew. She knew who Tibbs was and also knew enough not to interfere.

Emily turned her head and looked at the flowers as though they had become her entire world. Then, after another very long pause, she looked back at Tibbs. "Jerry! The driver was called Jerry. He said that they'd take me home and I heard one of them say, 'Right on, Jerry.'" That was all she had in her. She buried her face in her hands.

Virgil went close to her and bent over a little bit. "Thank you," he said. "Thank you very much."

He did not want to leave her that way, so he waited until she finally took her hands away from her face. "Does that help?" she asked.

Slowly Tibbs nodded. "Enough to send them all to prison, I think, where they belong."

The nurse came in once more. "Your father is here," she said. It was the moment to leave and Virgil took it. He did not introduce himself to the man in the hallway; it was not the right time to do so.

Suspect car number four was owned by Jerome Smith, aged nineteen, who had a record of two major sex offenses, among others.

Virgil passed the name identification back to the sheriff's detectives and then waited for results. Whatever there was to be learned would be back in his hands shortly. When he finally went home that night, he had the feeling that he had done a good day's work.

Miriam met him at the door. One quick look at her told him to steel himself for bad news; he was too experienced to expect anything else.

"Please come in, Virgil," she said, her voice very low and quiet. "We need you."

He complied and shut the door behind him. "What is it?" he asked.

Miriam drew a breath and then carefully paced her words. "I've been given a message. There's an uprising at home, a bad one, and my husband..."

She stopped and took a fresh grip on herself. "My husband is missing. As of right now, no one knows if he is still alive."

11

It was the beginning of the nightmare.

The first thing that caught his attention was the two children in the background. They were sober and quiet, so he knew they had been told well before his arrival. They were staying close to their mother, which made him feel a little like a hapless intruder.

A sense of frustration gripped him because there was so little he could do—he could not even touch her to tell her that he at least shared her great concern.

He sat down quietly and motioned to the children to come to him. When they obeyed, he talked to them calmly and quietly, holding Annette on his lap, with Pierre sitting by his side. He didn't try to discuss international politics; instead, he told them that now their father wanted them to do all that they could to help their mother. He was a very important man and they would have to measure up to what he expected of them. He pictured it as a kind of game—a game of being exceptionally good and not causing any trouble at all.

"Did you talk to daddy?" Annette asked.

It would have been easy to say yes to that, but he would not lie to the little girl. Instead he told her that grown-ups had a way of understanding each other that she would someday share. In the meantime, she could be sure that her daddy did want her to do just what he had said.

Pierre, despite his few years, was more mature. "You are a policeman," he said very carefully, finding the words as he needed them. "Please, will you help my father?"

That was easier. "To the very best of my ability," Virgil replied. That was completely true; the family was in his care and that much he could do in support of the man who was missing from his home thousands of miles away.

"Will you go and look for him?" The boy was grave and completely trusting.

Virgil looked up at Miriam, not knowing what to say. She came over and kneeled down so that she was on the same level with her children. "Your father has asked Mr. Tibbs to come here and protect us," she said. "He must stay here and do that, do you understand?"

When Pierre looked at her, steadily and without reaction, she spoke to him in another language, one that Tibbs could not understand. As he watched, both of the children responded; they came closer to her and then Pierre nodded gravely. At that moment Virgil felt himself completely lost. Miriam spoke with gentle, fluent ease, but the sounds were outside his ken and he sensed an additional barrier that he would never surmount.

Presently Miriam rose. She looked at him so trustfully that he wanted desperately to hold her and comfort her, if only for the sake of lending her his strength and support. He could not do that, even as a friend, but he could lend a hand. "You take care of the children," he said. "I'll get something to eat."

"Virgil, I'm sorry..."

He raised a hand and stopped her. "Perhaps Pierre will help me," he suggested.

When the boy came to him, Virgil took his hand and together they went into the kitchen. It was immaculately clean, but as he had already expected, Miriam had been much too engulfed in her grief and concern to have thought about food.

Tibbs was aware that he was no chef, but he had looked after himself for so long that he knew he would be able to get something together. There would be no TV dinners in that house, of course, but other things would be on hand. He opened the big refrigerator and explored.

He found bacon, tomatoes, and some sliced cheese, among other things. He searched until he located the bread; when he found a whole loaf, he knew that he could make a simple dish that might suffice.

It wasn't dinner and he knew it, but the less that he suggested anything was wrong the better it would be. He put open-faced toasted cheese sandwiches on a platter and set them in the middle of the table. As Miriam and Annette came in, he invited them to be seated.

It was a skimpy meal, but it succeeded. The children were delighted with the sandwiches; Miriam ate hers as though it had been prepared in a distinguished restaurant. She was unable to relax, even for a moment, but she ate two sandwiches and drank all of the milk that had been set before her. That in itself was a good sign. For the first time since he had come into the house, Virgil felt that he had been of some use.

When his private phone rang, he ran rapidly upstairs to take the call in his bedroom. McGowan was on the line. "I understand that some bad news was received today," he said.

"Yes, that's correct."

"How is the emotional climate where you are?"

"Grim."

"Should we be thinking in terms of some additional support?"

Virgil considered that for a moment and then answered. "You might consider Amiko."

"I take it you have confidence in her."

"Complete."

"I'll think about it and talk to some others."

"Thank you."

"Good-bye."

Tibbs hung up. Bob Nakamura already knew what was going on and his wife, Amiko, had two children of her own. He had suggested her because he sensed that at any time the presence of another woman might be close to essential.

At the preliminary hearing, Emily Myerson sat on the

witness stand, holding her emotions under tight rein, and did her best to tell the complete and absolute truth. She did not falter once from that determination and it was her total undoing.

The defense counsel began his questioning of her with every show of respect and consideration. "Miss Myerson," he began, "I'm very aware what a difficult thing this is for you and I promise that I will do all that I can to spare your feelings. There are a few things I must ask you, but I will try to stay away from the actual violence that was done to you."

"Thank you." Technically she should not have said that, but the judge let it pass.

"Now, Miss Myerson, as I understand it, you were walking home after seeing a movie when you were accosted."

"That's right."

"About what time was that?"

"Near eleven o'clock."

"Do you have a driver's license, Miss Myerson?"

"Yes, I do."

"And could you have had a car to take to the theater if you had wanted."

"I suppose so."

"But you chose to walk instead."

"Yes."

"Now, what was the condition of the street when you were on your way home?"

"I don't quite understand."

"Let me put it this way: Was it well lighted?"

"No, not very."

"Would it be fair to say that it was a dark street?"

"I guess so."

"Now, Miss Myerson, do you happen to have any male friends of about your own age who are black, good friends whom you would invite to your home?"

"I've met some black boys at school, but I don't know any of them very well."

"And you call them boys, I see. Now, Miss Myerson, I

see that you are wearing glasses. Do you wear them most of the time?"

"All of the time, unless I'm in bed or something like that."

"How well can you see without them?"

"Hardly at all. I don't have good eyes."

"I'm sorry, Miss Myerson, you're such a young person to have to wear glasses continuously. Now, were you wearing them when you were walking home from the movie?"

"Yes, I was. I said that I have to wear them all the time, except..."

The attorney cut her off. "Yes, yes, I fully understand that. Now you testified that you saw four young black men get out of a car somewhat ahead of you. Did you recognize any of them at that time?"

"No, they were strangers to me." The witness shuddered and showed signs of distress for a few moments. The judge leaned forward, but Emily recovered herself.

The defense attorney lowered his voice. "Now, Miss Myerson, you told us earlier that when these four young men approached you, one stood in front, one was on either side, and one remained in back. Is that right?"

"Yes."

"Did you look over at any time to the men on either side of you?"

"No."

"Did you turn and look at the man behind you?"

"No."

"All that you can say positively, then, is that you were accosted by four young black men?"

Emily flustered a little and showed some spunk. "That isn't true. I saw the one in front of me very well."

"Would you describe him, please."

"Well, he was about five feet nine or ten, with an Afro, medium build."

The attorney smiled, apparently a little amused. "Miss Myerson, that description is a very general one. In fact, it could apply to any of the four young men that are seated here in court. Isn't that so?"

The deputy district attorney spoke. "Objection."

"Sustained."

"Let me put it this way, then. Would the description you have just given me fit all four of the young men here?" He gestured.

Emily was honest. "I guess so. But how do you describe a face?"

"All right, tell me. How do you describe a face?"

Emily thought. "I don't know," she confessed.

"Now you got into the car with the four young men unwillingly, is that right?"

"Yes." She made that as strong as she dared.

"Were you actually shoved or pulled into the car?"

"No, but I was afraid that if I didn't get in…"

"Was it your belief at that time that the four young men would indeed drive you to your home?"

"I hoped they would. I didn't want them to think…"

"That's enough, Miss Myerson, just answer my questions, please. Now when you got into the car, were you still wearing your glasses?"

"Yes."

"Was it dark in the car?"

"Yes, very dark."

"Were you subsequently driven down any well-lighted streets?"

"No, they took me up into the hills…"

"I see. Now try and remember, at any time during the ride did you remove your glasses?"

"Yes, when I was jostled they fell off. One of the men picked them up, but he didn't give them back to me."

"Did you ask for them?"

"Yes, but he said I wouldn't need them."

"What did you think then?"

"I was terribly frightened."

"Now, Miss Myerson, I said that I didn't want to distress you by going into any of the details of the attack, so I will only ask you if you were without your glasses during the time that it happened."

"Yes, I was."

"You stated that you don't have any close male black friends your own age. In other words, you are not especially involved with the black community."

"No."

"And the place where you were attacked: was it also dark?"

"Yes."

"So in the dark, without your glasses, you were not able to see clearly. Is that right?"

Emily hung her head. She knew that she had been trapped, and she did not know when she had gone wrong. She had told nothing but the truth. She had believed that the truth would be her protector, but it had betrayed her.

"Now, Miss Myerson," the voice went on, pillorying her with every word. "You only saw your attackers on a dark street, in a dark car, and later, in a very dark place. You said that you did not see them clearly on the street, that you never looked at three of them. In the car you lost your glasses and, by your own admission, you cannot see clearly without them. The description you gave the court of the one man you did see was so vague it could be applied to any one, or all four, of the defendants. Can you now say that you can positively identify all four of the young men seated here as the ones who attacked you? Is there any possible way you can do that without going back on your own testimony?"

There was a long pause. Emily was shaken to the point where, for a moment, she didn't care anymore. And the way out was in front of her. "I guess not," she said.

The judge looked down at her with pity. She had been on the bench more than twenty years and she knew that the four accused men were guilty as surely as if their names had been written on stone tablets and handed down from Mount Sinai. But she also knew that the victim's admission that she could not positively identify the four suspects as her attackers would make a conviction during the trial phase impossible.

She excused the witness, with the thanks of the court, and watched as the poor, innocent, and truthful girl was escorted out. Then she turned back to the business at hand, knowing there would be a motion to dismiss all charges and that she would most reluctantly have to grant it.

The body of Jerome Smith—burglar, robber, addict, and rapist—was found in the Arroyo Seco quite by accident less than a week later. He had been dead for several hours, apparently having been killed sometime during the early evening. A wide piece of adhesive tape had been pasted across his mouth and his throat had been slashed by a very sharp instrument almost literally from ear to ear.

It was not until the body had been placed on the autopsy table that it was discovered that his testicles had been crushed in a manner that must have caused the most excruciating pain imaginable.

12

Lieutenant Dick Smith was a very tall man, well built, and with a deceptively amiable face. One of his great professional assets was his unflappability: He could walk into almost any situation and handle it without the least evidence of being upset or annoyed. He had once responded in the field to a vicious fight going on in a house filled with Mexican illegals. He had calmly wandered in, taken knives away from two of the more aggressive men, quieted down some screaming females, and restored order in a matter of three or four minutes. The fact that none of the Mexicans concerned had any knowledge of English, and that Smith knew no Spanish, hadn't appeared to matter. His personality had been enough.

He sat in his office, the door shut, with Bob Nakamura and Virgil Tibbs. "I want your thoughts on the two homicides we've had recently," he said in his very easy manner. "Let me have any ideas that may have come to you, even if they don't seem to make sense."

Bob looked at Virgil, who knew that he would have to pick up the ball.

"I'm coming from left field," he said, "but here's how I see it. The two killings are related and I think they're the work of the same people. At least two, possibly three or more, persons were involved and there may be a much larger organization behind them. The fact that both of the victims were young black men has a definite bearing. The actual killers are probably based in Pasadena, but I suspect that they're highly mobile and may hit again in some other jurisdiction. So we may be working with other agencies before we're through. I think the killers are not black themselves. Also, they're not motivated by any personal injuries done to them; they're taking revenge on behalf of the community."

"Vigilantes, in other words," Smith said.

"You could call them that," Tibbs agreed, "which will make pinning them down that much harder. Also, I don't believe that they are the kind of people who act impulsively; they're inclined to plan each step carefully. I see them as intelligent and resourceful."

Smith turned to the Nisei detective. "Anything to add to that, Bob?"

"One small observation: Both of the victims were felons dangerous to society; neither one of them had any redeeming virtues that I know of. I agree with Virg that whoever killed them considered that he was doing society a favor."

"You can see a group of vigilantes, then."

"Yes."

The lieutenant went back to Virgil. "Suppose you fill me in on how you reached your conclusions."

Tibbs reverted to his quietest manner. "Let me start with the relationship between the two crimes. They were distinctive in that they were both executions. Tompkins, you remember, was hanged. Consider this: two men, for the sake of argument, got hold of him and decided that they were going to do him in. There are a lot of relatively easy ways. They could shoot him, stab him, or even drop him off a good high bridge—we have several of those around. But instead they went to the considerable trouble to hang him in the classic manner; and incidentally, they used the right kind of noose. The only difference is they didn't use the drop that brings instant and painless death; they let him strangle, which is a lot tougher way to go.

"Smith, the rapist, was also executed. I came to that conclusion almost as soon as I saw the body."

"Explain," Smith invited.

"His mouth was taped and then his throat was cut. That

had to be the sequence, because there wouldn't be any point in taping his mouth *after* opening up his windpipe. Actually, I believe his mouth was covered to prevent him from crying out when his testicles were crushed. That particular type of injury was probably suggested by the crime he committed.

"About the execution: The people who killed him had a very sharp implement that wasn't a razor blade—it went much too deep. They could have easily stabbed him and it would have been logical for them under the circumstances. But they cut his throat instead. They didn't just want him dead; they wanted him to die in a particular manner. And he did."

"Then it's your thinking that the two are related because of the execution techniques," Smith said. "I can buy that."

"There's more, Dick. Both Tompkins and Smith committed major crimes and were subsequently released—Tompkins on bail and Smith at the preliminary hearing. They were both clearly guilty: Tompkins was definitely IDed as one of the bandits who robbed the market. Smith got off because the defense attorney managed to shake up the victim enough to make her go back on her own identification of the suspects. The judge knew the score, but she also knew that no conviction was possible, so she followed the law and released them."

"What do you see in the fact that both victims were black?" the lieutenant asked. The question did not embarrass him; the Pasadena Police were beyond the point where a man's ethnic origin cut any ice at all.

"Most responsible leaders of the black community are concerned over the high crime rate among their young people, just as the Chicano community is trying desperately to find an answer to their youth gangs. I don't intend to go into the possible reasons why these conditions exist, but they're a major problem. So on a statistical or probability basis, the fact that both of the victims were young black criminals doesn't mean too much. But suppose that there was a group, large or small, that resented blacks, particularly those who are criminals. Suppose they blame the whole community for the actions of a few. A black pistol-whips a white man; the former gets killed—or his partner does. Four young blacks rape a white girl, and one of them is executed. Do you see the pattern?"

"By the way, what happened to the other three rape suspects?" Bob asked.

"Two of them hopped a bus for Detroit as soon as they heard about Smith—I got that from the sheriff's people. The fourth one is in jail; there was a warrant out on him for child molestation."

"And Tompkins' partner—the other holdup man?"

"In custody, which may be a good thing for him."

The lieutenant returned to the main topic. "Do you see a connection between the fact that in each instance a white person was attacked by blacks?"

"No," Tibbs answered. "I have a gut feeling that if Emily Myerson had been black, it would have gone the same way."

"Would she have been avenged so savagely?"

"Yes, because a rapist is a rapist no matter who his victim is. Everybody despises him."

"What's your point of attack?" the lieutenant asked.

"I want to find out from our intelligence guys all that I can about hate groups in or around the city," Virgil answered. "Mild or aggressive. The American Nazi Party, the KKK, whatever they have or I can dig up. That's where I'll start."

"I agree," Bob said.

Smith bought that. "All right, both of you get going along those lines. The chief wants you relieved of everything else for the time being, so turn your other files over to me; I'll reassign them. Do you need anything else?"

"How about an expense account?" Bob quipped.

Smith took him seriously. "I'll approve whatever is necessary. You be the judge."

At that moment they both realized *how* serious the lieutenant was; he had never been known to miss a joke before.

Dr. William Pierce Smedley sat in his office, surrounded by a massive clutter that reached almost to the ceiling in many places. As he perched in his swivel chair, he kept constantly rotating it a few degrees, first one way and then the other. He seemed incapable of sitting still. He held a pencil between his fingers, one hand supporting each end, and kept it in almost constant motion. He was a small, peppery man who wore a coat and tie despite the lack of adequate air conditioning so that at any moment he would be prepared to keep an appointment with destiny.

If his motions were a trifle more intense than usual, it was because he was being questioned by two investigators from the police department, who sat facing him, neither of whom met with his full approval. However, they were on the right side of the fence as far as he was concerned, and that helped somewhat to erase the unfavorable impression that their visible ethnic origin had provoked.

When he spoke his voice was dry and static, but a great deal of nervous energy was behind it. "I'll give it to you right off the top," he declared. "I've got a lot to do and I'm seriously behind schedule, but I won't refuse to co-operate with the police. I want to impress on you both very firmly that we are a completely law-abiding organization. We do our work within the framework that's permitted. We're sponsoring some legislation to give us additional breathing room, but until it's passed we'll go on just as we're doing now."

"That's most important, Dr. Smedley," Bob Nakamura said with every evidence of sincerity. "I want you to know that we appreciate it very much."

"I'm glad you have the sense to," Smedley snapped. "Not everyone does. All right." He stopped the motion of his chair and held onto the edge of his desk as though he expected it to attempt to fly away. "We are patriots here. If you want to read a statement of our philosophy, you can go back to Tom Paine at the time of the Revolution. We believe in America and we intend to defend it against all enemies—foreign and domestic. Tell me, when you were sworn in as policemen, you took a vow to do exactly that, didn't you?"

"Absolutely," Tibbs answered him. "And they never let us forget it."

Smedley eased the pressure of his fingers and relaxed to a small degree. "I'm certainly glad to hear that," he conceded. "Now, we are accused of being racist here, but that isn't true. Any man who wants to stand up for his country, who will fight for it if need be, and will help to keep America strong is all right with us. What we are against, and what we're fighting against, are the millions of illegal foreigners who come in here, crowd out Americans from the places they live, take their jobs, and then breed like flies. Have you got any idea how many kids an average Mexican family has? And blacks are the same way—they have more kids than the white population can afford to feed. I'm sorry to say that to your face, Tibbs, but it's a fact and you know it. And you know, too, that by the year 1986 this is going to be a black nation unless we do something about it. You're educated, that's different, but how about the sprawling masses that never got past the fourth grade? Fifteen kids per black family and less than two in the white community. You see which way we're going?"

Virgil nodded to show that he had listened; it was a convenient technique that didn't require him to give any other response. "Just how are you going about your program, Dr. Smedley?" he asked.

"Fair question. All right, glad to answer." The swinging back and forth began once more. "First, we want everyone—every responsible person—to understand what's going on. Then we're promoting a major birth control program in the ghetto areas. We run right into the Catholics here, of course, but we're making a lot of progress just the same. One or two kids per family—fine. Fifteen is out of the question. Their parents can't support them, most of the time they aren't wanted, and we're running out of resources to care for them.

"We're campaigning to have the millions of illegal Mexican aliens in this country sent home where they belong.

89

If they want to come here, let them go through the proper legal channels, the way so many others have to, the way my father and mother did. One exception: We agree to permit seasonal farm workers to stay when their help is needed.

"*But*"—the word came out with astonishing force from the small man behind the desk—"we don't condone violence, or murder, or even intimidation. We work for legal evictions of illegal aliens. We sponsor birth control forums and distribute literature. Starting next month, we are going to sell birth control devices in the poor and minority communities at cost; for those who can't pay, we'll give them away. And we have a speakers bureau that will provide free lectures on Americanism and what the traditions of this country mean. Don't mix us up with the Birchers, even though we agree on some things. We saw a major problem coming; we're meeting it head on."

"Dr. Smedley," Tibbs said, "what you've told us is very important for us to know. Now, as an expert in the field of social action, can you suggest any group, or groups, who aren't satisfied to follow your example, who might, in fact, resort to the violence you have ruled out?"

Smedley thought before he gave his answer. "I wouldn't care to say."

"You understand," Bob Nakamura added, "that we are consulting you in absolute confidence."

Smedley took hold of the corner of his desk again and allowed his visitors to see how hard he was thinking. "I've heard of a man named Ryan," he said slowly. "You might have a few words with him. I'm sure you can find him."

"Emmett Ryan?" Tibbs asked.

Smedley looked at him sharply. "I see the police are aware of what's going on. That isn't his real name, of course, but it's what he calls himself. You might find it interesting to look up his real name—if you can."

Tibbs stood up and Bob followed suit. "By any chance, sir," Virgil asked, "would you happen to know what it is?"

Smedley shook his head sharply. "I'm sorry, but that you're going to have to find out for yourselves."

*   *   *

"What do you think?" Bob asked when they were back in the car.

"He's a gutsy little guy; he didn't hesitate to insult both of us, but he also declared his support for the police—several times, as a matter of fact."

"I caught that," Bob said, "but it could just be lip service. He may hate our guts because we're cops."

"Did you read him as a violent person?" Tibbs asked.

"No, I can't say that I did. According to Jerry in intelligence, he hasn't done anything so far that would allow us to bust him. It's true that his outfit is sponsoring birth control programs in the ghetto areas. Some pretty responsible people have endorsed that idea—at least in principle. Others, of course, oppose it."

"What about Ryan?"

Tibbs swung the car smoothly round a corner, heading back toward headquarters. "He's a better candidate, certainly. Ever since he was busted for that big weapons cache out in the desert he's been pretty quiet, but he believes in violence. Nobody doubts that."

"When do we see him?"

"You just asked the pertinent question. Right after lunch."

It was not to be. Shortly after noon, three bandits successfully robbed a filling station on the east side of the city, shot the manager, who had tried to go for a weapon in his office, and made their escape. It was a brutal, savage crime and the police department pulled out all the stops. Every detective who could be spared was put on the case. There were a number of fragile leads, but every one of them was followed up to the end. Virgil Tibbs worked all through the night and didn't get home until daylight.

Miriam had been waiting for him, sleeping on the couch in the living room. She had set some food out in the kitchen for him, but when he at last came into the room, dog tired, he couldn't think of food. He dropped into a chair out of sheer exhaustion, loosened his tie, and leaned back with his eyes shut.

"Are you all right?" Miriam asked.

"Yes, just tired. It's been an awful night."

"Was Bob with you?"

"Some of the time. I've got to be back by noon, but I'm too beat to go to bed."

Miriam knelt down and took off his shoes. Then she helped him out of his coat. "I know," she said. "My husband often comes home the same way. Completely exhausted."

That roused Tibbs a little. "Any word?" he asked.

Miriam shook her head silently, her eyes visibly moist.

Tired as he was, Virgil tried to find the right words to reassure her. As a policeman, he knew that she had ample cause for concern; heads of state did not disappear that way without a strong likelihood of some kind of foul play. But he would never tell her that, although he realized that she knew it already. He tried to tell himself that her husband was alive and well, removed to some safe place where he was surrounded by his loyal supporters, and well protected.

"There is some news," Miriam said. "It isn't very good. I was told last night that there are some Cuban troops in my country. I have no idea how many."

Virgil Tibbs did not need any more bad news. "I'm going to bed," he announced. He climbed slowly up to his room, shut the door, and was out of his clothes in a matter of seconds. He put his gun at his bedside, where he would be able to reach it quickly in any emergency, and fell into bed. When the downstairs phone rang again, he did not even hear it.

13

A solid week of quiet, intensive work came to an end with almost nothing definitely accomplished except in a purely negative sense. Interviews with the spokesmen of a number of suspect organizations were inconclusive. Some of the interviews were gladly, even eagerly, given while others proved very difficult. Three different groups flatly refused to receive a police representative and another told Tibbs that they would talk only with a white person. The sum and substance of it all was close to nil.

On Saturday Virgil took his adoptive family to the Los Angeles Zoo. He had recognized that the children in particular were growing increasingly restless, but before they set out he took some careful precautions. He had brought home blue jeans for the children to wear. Per his instruction, Miriam wore as ordinary an outfit as she could produce, while he chose a conventional sport shirt and a pair of slacks he frequently wore for doing odd jobs around the house.

"You are not to speak to us when other people are close by," he instructed Pierre and Annette. "You have accents that would tell almost anyone that you are foreign-born. Right now we don't want to call attention to that."

"We understand," Pierre said gravely.

"I have instructed them that they are to call you 'daddy' at all times," Miriam added.

"Good. Now I want to remind you of the cover story just in case we run into someone I know. You are the ex-wife of a wealthy French merchant; you divorced him because of his constant drinking and abuse of your children. You have means of your own and were traveling in Nepal when we met in Katmandu—I was over there on the Doris Friedkin case. You came here at my invitation and we are living together. We plan to marry after your divorce is final."

"You need not fear that I will forget," Miriam said, a little formally. "That story was my idea. They wanted to make me the widow of a French policeman killed in the line of duty, but I told them I don't know enough about police work; if I met your colleagues, they would see through me. I am happy to appear as your present mistress and prospective bride."

Tibbs pressed his lips together for a moment while he reminded himself who she really was. "I hope it won't be necessary," he said.

The day at the zoo was a complete success. The children took to their new clothing as though they had worn jeans all their lives, while Miriam was appropriately inconspicuous. Nevertheless, she drew more than her share of inquisitive glances; Tibbs noted them all, particularly the fact that the most appreciative stares seemed to come from white men. He stayed as close to his charge and responsibility as he could; he was disturbed only when it seemed to him that she had remained in the ladies' room an inordinately long time. When she did reappear, he was immediately relieved.

Despite her abilities as a gourmet cook, Miriam ate a hot dog and some potato chips for lunch with every sign of relish. As the afternoon wore on, the fantasy that they were actually a family on an outing grew stronger; the children addressed him very naturally as "daddy," while Miriam held his arm with just the right amount of possessiveness.

They did not see, or meet, anyone whom Tibbs knew or could recognize. If any other agency was covering them, the job was so expert that he never detected it. On the way home he wanted to stop and take them to dinner at the Salt Shaker, but that was a code seven stop and some other policemen were almost certain to be there. Instead he bought a large container of fried chicken to spare Miriam the work of fixing a meal. When his private phone rang an hour later, he reported to the chief that the outing had gone well and without incident.

The atmosphere was very different on Monday morning at headquarters. Tibbs had been over the crime reports and there was nothing that he could tie in with the two execution-type slayings to which he had been assigned. No jurisdiction in the Los Angeles basin reported a homicide or any other crime that suggested a connection.

One thing did interest him: There had been an armed robbery on Saturday night not too far from where he was living. It had been pulled by a salt-and-pepper team—two blacks and a white. It had been a vicious operation and the filling-station manager, who was the victim, felt that he had escaped with his life by the narrowest of margins. "I gave them all they asked for and I gave it to them fast," he was quoted as saying in the crime report. "Then I handed them my wallet just so they would feel I wasn't holding out on anything."

"Why do you think they let you go?" he had been asked.

"Because I co-operated, because they wore ski masks, and because I told them I had done hard time myself. That seemed to convince them I wouldn't snitch."

"Have you actually been in prison?"

"No, but I'd thought about being held up someday and I had that story ready."

There was nothing whatever new that might help in solving the two cases in which Tibbs was most interested.

From his desk he took out a packet of three-by-five-inch plain white filing cards. For the next forty minutes he was busy writing different points of information on them, one pertinent fact on each card. When he had finished, he laid them all out in a pattern on the top of his desk. There were gaping holes in his design, pieces of information that he did not have, but he was able to see what he had available in a controlled sequence.

Bob Nakamura had seen him do that many times before.

When the layout was finished, Tibbs sat perfectly still and studied it, noting the gaps and establishing the continuity wherever any was visible. After a few minutes he wrote on three more cards and added them to his layout. For more than an hour he devoted himself entirely to his display of cards and the data that they represented. Then, when he had gone as far as he could, he gathered them all up in order, put a rubber band around them, and stored them carefully in his desk.

"What have you got?" Bob asked.

"I'm doing this one on probabilities," Virgil answered. "I have some things that are definite and some that I've had to guess at, logical deductions that I believe in. But, remember, even Sherlock Holmes was wrong on two or three occasions. So I have to allow some leeway for error. But it's just possible that I see some light."

"Definite suspects?"

"Possibly, but I've got to check a lot more first."

On the following day the salt-and-pepper bandits hit again, this time in Glendale. Again a filling station was the target and the two employees on duty became casualties. One of them tried to get to a concealed holdup alarm and was shot through the kneecap. The other offered no resistance at all, but while he held his hands in the air he was viciously kicked in the groin; when he fell to the ground in agony, another member of the team kicked him hard in the face. He was still screaming in pain when the paramedics arrived and he had to be restrained on the gurney while he was being transported.

Within an hour after the attack, a team of two detectives from Glendale came to Pasadena so that MO information could be exchanged. One minor point came from a witness: The white member of the bandit team had delivered the face kick after the employee had been so badly hurt that he was lying on the ground in severe pain.

Lieutenant Smith was shorthanded. He had been keeping Tibbs and Nakamura entirely on the execution cases, but he could no longer afford that luxury. He assigned them to work with Glendale on the salt-and-pepper bandits.

There was considerable discussion of how the problem should be approached. All available snitches would be checked, all witnesses interviewed in depth, and the MO files searched for possible matches. Tibbs also sent for the latest prison release records to determine who had just come out and might be part of the three-man team. In particular, he checked for any parolees or other releases of known close friends of two different races. The prison gangs mitigated against that, so if he did turn up something it could be highly significant.

He put out the word to the patrol forces to watch for any suspicious vehicles that contained two or more men of different races, excluding Orientals. He considered it quite possible that the white man might be a Mexican, but that was no more than a guess. Viciousness in criminals was prevalent in persons of all ethnic backgrounds, but because of the Mexican prison gangs he decided to play the percentages.

Since ski masks had been used again on the second hit, there were no descriptions. The clothing worn by the bandits had been so ordinary that nothing useful could be gained from what little was known.

At the end of a very trying day, Tibbs went back to his temporary home. As he drove there, he fervently hoped that there would be some good news concerning President Motamboru; Miriam's almost desperate concern added materially to his burden.

She greeted him at the door. One look at her face told him that his hopes had been unjustified, but she gave him the news anyway. She had received one phone call telling her that nothing definite had been learned except that the Cuban troops in her country were waging a relentless campaign and a large number of people had been killed.

She still had dinner ready. At the table the children were very silent and Tibbs hardly knew what he was putting into his mouth. For the first time he had the feeling that he was in over his head. He could not leave his work at the office and go back to his apartment in relative peace. There was no peace for him and he feared a ring on the phone more than ever.

After a restless night, he got up early without disturbing Miriam, ate a bowl of cereal, and left for his office. A small idea was germinating in the back of his mind and he wanted to check it out.

It did not take him long to locate Rubin Goldfarb, the owner of the store that had been held up by Leonard Tompkins and his companion. For that offense, presumably, Tompkins had paid with his life at the end of a hangman's rope.

Mr. Goldfarb was not yet in his office, but the answering service promised to give him the message to call Mr. Tibbs at the Pasadena Police Department as soon as he came in.

Next he turned his attention to the release reports he had requested, which were now on his desk. As usual, the parole board had been more than liberal in its release of convicted felons back into society. He had never been able to escape the conviction that if the judge said an offense was worth five years in prison, the person sentenced should serve five years. If the court felt that the penalty should be less, then a lighter sentence could be pronounced. As it was, life imprisonment actually meant a maximum of seven years and it could, under some circumstances, be even less. He recognized that he had a hardnosed attitude, but he had seen too many crime victims who had been hit by parolees. If the penalties were too lenient, then the price of lawlessness dropped and the risk to the criminal was reduced to the point where robbery and other crimes might appear to be an attractive profession.

He checked the release lists for the past six months, looking for people who might possibly make up the salt-and-pepper team that had already pulled two major jobs in quick succession. The MOs used suggested experience and that, in turn, suggested persons released, either on parole or upon completion of their sentences. He also circulated other jurisdictions for a similar series of crimes. The salt-and-pepper aspect was a little unusual and that, at least, gave him something with which to work.

Rubin Goldfarb called and offered to meet with Tibbs at any mutually convenient time. Since Goldfarb had his office in Pasadena, Virgil suggested that he would be right over. Goldfarb agreed.

If Tibbs had had any preconceived ideas as to what sort of man he would be meeting, he did not reveal them when he shook hands with the blond, handsome six-footer who received him with every sign of cordiality. Goldfarb was a young man—thirty-five at the most—who had about him the air of the man who is almost universally successful with women. It was Tibbs's first impression that if he ever slept a night alone, it was by his own choice. He even felt for a moment a touch of envy.

Goldfarb's office was ample but not showy. It was the office of a man who used it to conduct business and not to impress his visitors with either its dimensions or its decor. Tibbs also noted that his host was very well dressed; his expensive sportswear was subdued and in the very best of taste. In view of Goldfarb's youth, either he had to be a near business genius or else he had come into money by inheritance or, possibly, by gift.

Tibbs began the conversation in a quiet, factual manner. "Mr. Goldfarb, this concerns a holdup of one of your stores in which your clerk, Willis Raymond, was pistol-whipped. Are you familiar with what happened after that?"

Goldfarb picked up a cigarette, toyed with it, and then put it down again. "I'm quitting," he explained. "To answer your question: obviously I've followed all the developments that have been made public. I know that the holdup men were promptly caught, that they were released on bail or some other way, and that one of them was found a few days later. It was a bizarre thing; he had been hanged."

"In some respects quite professionally," Tibbs added. "We don't as yet know by whom. I understand that you own several stores."

"Yes, nine to be exact. They aren't my principal business activity, but they are profitable to a limited degree. We have to charge two or three cents more for almost every item and that isn't a convenience surcharge; it's the cost of insurance. The rates we have to pay are very high. I may have to use armed guards to protect our personnel and our customers."

"A lot of firms have done that," Tibbs commented.

"I know. As I recall, a private guard shot two bandits at the risk of his own life a couple of years ago."

"That's right," Virgil said. "We gave him a police commendation. Have any of your other stores been hit?"

Goldfarb pricked up his ears at that one. "Three attempts in the last four months. In only one case did the bandits get any money, but the risk is high and my people know it."

"How do you manage to keep your employees?"

"By means of a very simple principle: Automobile drivers think that accidents always happen to the other guy. Of course we do the best we can to protect our people. We have elaborate alarm systems and the criminal community seems to know that. Also, we will prosecute; we have signs posted in all our stores to that effect. And I do pay good salaries, considering the type of work involved."

"In your opinion, Mr. Goldfarb, are you being hit more often than other operators of the same type of store?"

"To be honest about it, Tibbs, we're all being hit far too often. We know the police protection is good, particularly in Pasadena, but it still isn't enough to stop the crime. And it's getting worse."

"One more question: Have you any suggestion to make concerning who might have hung Leonard Tompkins?"

"No, I have no idea at all. I will say this off the record: He did everyone a favor and I can't wish too hard that you'll catch him. The man who was hanged deserved it, in my opinion."

Virgil didn't comment. Instead he said the appropriate things and went back to his car.

When he returned to his office, he filled out two more filing cards and added them to his pack.

After his usual lunch, consisting of a sandwich and a milk shake, Tibbs took an unmarked car and drove down the Harbor Freeway to San Pedro. There he talked to several marina operators and three different ship supply stores. Back in his car once more, he filled out four more cards. As he drove back to Pasadena, he realized how much times had changed. One marina operator had paid him the high compliment of suggesting that he might like to buy a boat.

The next morning he went to the office of the Los Angeles County Coroner and talked with the pathologist who had performed the autopsy on the body of Jerome Smith, the rapist. "I understand that his testicles were crushed," Tibbs began.

"That's right, they were," the doctor confirmed.

"In your opinion, were they smashed by a sudden blow or were they slowly crushed?"

"I can be pretty definite on that. It was a single blow, or, rather, two blows. It's impossible to say whether or not the blows were delivered in rapid succession. If they weren't..."

"In any event, the pain must have been excruciating."

"So much so that the victim may well have passed out."

"I was just coming to that. It is possible, then, that he may have been unconscious when his throat was cut."

"It's a better than even bet that he was, considering what had been done to him."

"One more question, doctor: Could he have cut his own throat?"

"You mean to escape the pain? A kind of forced suicide? No, I can't see that at all. Also, it was one long, even stroke; no man could have done that to himself, although I've seen some who tried."

Tibbs expressed his thanks and once more stopped in his car to fill out two of his filing cards. The data he needed were beginning to come to the surface. He still had a long way to go, but he was at least building a foundation.

When he returned to the station, he was intercepted by Shelley Larson, one of the police clerks who manned the front desk. "You have a message," she said, and handed him a slip of paper. "From a citizen. She asked that you call her back as soon as you got in."

"Did she ask for me by name?"

"No, but she did ask to speak to the detective who was in charge of the case—the one about the man found with his throat cut."

Tibbs was back in his office and on the phone within two minutes. It could be a break. Sometimes the most difficult cases were solved when a citizen came forward with a piece of information.

The phone rang several times before it was answered. When an elderly feminine voice said "Hello," Virgil's hopes sank a notch; it sounded like another case of a senior citizen who had had a dream in which the guilty person was revealed.

"This is Virgil Tibbs at the Pasadena Police," he said. "I understand that you have some information for us."

"Yes, that's right." The voice gained a little in strength and assurance. "I would have called in sooner, but, you see, we've been away. We have a motor home, a very nice one, and we like to take trips all around California. Don't you think California is beautiful, Mr. Tibbs?"

"I certainly do," Tibbs agreed. "I wouldn't want to live anywhere else."

That encouraged his informant, which was precisely what he had hoped to do.

"This is Mrs. Bennett. Mrs. Homer Bennett. What I wanted to tell you was that we've been away and we haven't seen the papers, so we didn't understand, you see?"

Tibbs didn't see, but he knew better than to show the slightest impatience. When Mrs. Homer Bennett did finally come to the point, she might very well have something important to report. He had already decided that she was probably not a ding; although she rambled, she was following a logical mental pattern.

"I understand, of course," Tibbs answered.

"Oh, I'm so glad. Well, now, we were driving down in the Arroyo Seco. We had had our motor home in the garage in preparation for our trip. They were late finishing the work, so after dinner we took a cab to the garage to get the motor home. My husband and I, that is. Is all this clear?"

"Entirely clear, Mrs. Bennett. Please continue."

"Well, we were coming back through the arroyo because it's the most convenient way to get home. We live up toward La Canada. I'll be glad to give you our address if you want it. My husband was driving and I was sitting in one of the armchairs in the living room part of the motor home—that's right behind the driver's section and in front of the door. I didn't have the inside light on, so I could see out very well. And the visibility from a motor home is much better than it is from a passenger car; you sit a lot higher and the windows are much bigger—at least it seems that way."

"I quite understand," Virgil said.

"You know, I thought that talking with the police was going to be so difficult, but it isn't at all. I wish now that I'd called you before, the time last year that Mrs. Metcalf was robbed and I thought I saw the burglars, at least I did have the license number. But anyway, as I said, the lights were off and I was looking out the window so I could see very well even though it was dark. That's when I saw those three men."

"Just where did you see them, Mrs. Bennett?"

"Right where the body was found, that's the point! You see, there was a map in the paper showing the place; it was marked with a black cross. I know it's right where we were passing by. Otherwise, why would three men come out of the wooded area that way? Or the bushes—or whatever. Anyway, they came out and I saw them clearly. And I saw a car parked there that had to be theirs."

"That's excellent, Mrs. Bennett. Can you tell me anything about the car?"

"Well, it was a sedan, kind of a dirty gray, I think, but the light wasn't very good, you understand. I really don't know anything about cars, but it wasn't a shiny new one—an old one, I think, but not too old…?"

Tibbs remained calm. "Thank you, I have that. Now can you describe the three men?"

"Well, not exactly. I mean. I can't tell you just what they looked like. They were young men, I'd say strong—you know, the kind that might be able to play games and things like that. They weren't frail or fat..."

Virgil was more than happy. His informant might be garrulous, but he knew that she was truthful and not imagining things. And she had given him a partial description of the car and supplied the fact that there had been three youthful men. It wasn't a lot, but it was something.

"What you are telling me is very valuable, Mrs. Bennett," he said into the phone. "I can't tell you how much we appreciate your coming forward like this. Now can you tell me anything else about the three men, anything at all?"

"Well, yes. And that's really why I called, you see. Because I did read about that holdup at the filling station; it's terrible the way that crime is gaining on us so fast. That's why I think a responsible citizen has to help when she can. Anyway, to get back to the three men, it was like the way the paper described the holdup men. You see, Mr. Tibbs, I remember them because two of them were black—there are a lot of blacks in that part of town, you know—and the third one was white. I could see that very clearly."

14

Virgil was still seated at his desk, deep in thought, when Bob Nakamura came in. The Nisei detective sat down and waited for his partner to speak. He knew Tibbs very well and understood his moods.

"Anything new?" The words were peculiarly flat, which told Bob a lot.

He shook his head. "I've been out doorbell-ringing all day, trying to get a witness, any kind of a witness. Nothing. Nobody saw the bandits except the immediate victims. And they've been interviewed to the point where I'm sure they don't have anything more for us. They all agree that it was two blacks and a white man, they could see that through the ski masks. One witness thought he saw a small tattoo on the forearm of one of the blacks, but he isn't too confident."

"Any more make on the vehicle?"

"Dark sedan, no make or model. Not new, not old. One witness thought it was tan, two others called it gray."

"Three," Tibbs said.

Bob came to life. "You've got something!"

"That's the hell of it," Virgil said. "It adds up one way, and not at all the other."

"Give, man, give."

"A citizen called in. She saw three men leaving the site where the body of Jerome Smith was found."

"The man with the ventilated throat."

"Right. It was night, but she claims to have seen clearly

that two of them were black and one white."

"How does the time check out?"

"Right on the button, according to the coroner's estimated time of death. She also saw a vehicle that she described as a dirty gray."

Bob was giving his full attention. "I see several things. First, salt-and-pepper teams like that aren't too common. Second, the team we've been chasing is made up of established hardcore baddies. They're violent and sadistic. Smith had his balls crushed; that's about as sadistic as you can get. Third, as far as it goes, the vehicle checks out."

Virgil put his elbows on his desk and rested his chin on his palms. "All that's true, but look at the other side. The salt-and-pepper team are bandits. Leonard Tompkins, who got hanged, was a bandit. Why would one bandit crew take out another?"

"Territorial infringement. Suppose the salt-and-pepper team set up something and word got around enough that Tompkins and company decided to have a go at it themselves."

"No, the word wouldn't get around like that. Territorial infringement—a bare possibility. But that doesn't explain the job done on Jerome Smith. That looks like revenge all the way. I've checked out Mr. Myerson, the father of the victim, and he's Mr. Clean."

"Boyfriend?"

"No go. The victim is a Plain Jane but a hell of a gutsy kid. I'm for her."

"Virg, is there any way that she was picked ahead of time for the rape?"

"None that I can see, she was a target of opportunity. If she were a living, breathing gorgeous doll, I might think so, but she probably hasn't had a half dozen dates in her life." Tibbs turned and looked at Nakamura face to face. "Now, I see certain links between the two execution killings, but assume for the moment that there aren't any. Jerome Smith was a sadistic rapist and it cost him. It was his body that my informant saw three men leaving. Oh, hell, you know what I mean. She saw three men leaving

106

the area where Smith's body was later found. So here's the big question: Why would three known holdup men go to work on Smith as someone did?"

Bob came to life. "Got it! Look for the connection with Emily Myerson, the rape victim. A brother, anyone who knew her. The white man is the best bet, unless she had close friends who were black."

"I thought of that, of course," Tibbs responded, "but I can't make it swing. She just doesn't have any close friends. A few girls like her, but she isn't date bait. She was a virgin before the attack. Does that tell you anything?"

"Plain and principled."

"Something like that. She isn't pretty, she doesn't have an appealing figure, and she doesn't put out. Add that she's naive and you can see her sitting home a lot on Saturday nights."

"Virg, how many three-man salt-and-pepper teams have you known who operate in this area?"

Tibbs got up and walked over to the window of his office. "I've got some good snitches and I've talked to them all. They never heard of one before now. So the answer to your question is either one or two. Two would be a helluva co-incidence and I don't believe in them."

"Neither do I," Bob said, "but they have been known to happen."

At 9:37 that evening, a small supermarket in Azusa was suddenly and professionally held up. Three man in ski masks burst into the store and, with guns drawn, demanded that the few persons in the store freeze. A woman shopper took one step and a bullet hit her in the upper shoulder.

"I said freeze!" The man in the ski mask left no doubt that he meant it. The manager was only a few inches from the silent robbery alarm, but if the store had been cased, the bandits would know that and any move on his part could mean death. He remained motionless and prayed fervently that he would get out of it alive.

One of the bandits, a black man, vaulted over the check-out counter, knocked the checker out of the way, and rapidly emptied the contents of the cash register into a paper sack. While the white masked man held everyone motionless, his two black partners emptied the two other registers—all this occurring one half hour before the receipts would have been taken out and put in the store's safe until the following morning's regular pickup.

The bandits were out of the store in less than two minutes. Seconds later a car could be heard burning rubber getting out of the parking lot.

The first Azusa unit rolled onto the lot code three less than two minutes after that, but it was already too late. For the better part of an hour the market parking lot held many official vehicles; an ambulance had come and gone, but there was little that could be done. It was determined that two of the bandits had been black, the third white. No one had seen the car they had used. The cash loss was unusually large; in addition, the shopper who had been shot had been taken away screaming that she was going to sue the store for fifty million dollars.

The Azusa police recognized the makeup of the bandit team and promptly notified both Pasadena and Glendale of what had gone down. All patrol units were told to look for a gray car, or any car, with three men, two black and one white. It was an almost hopeless search. By dawn it was recognized that the hit had been completely successful. There was not one new piece of information that might help in establishing a pattern, except for the fact that the team appeared to operate only on the north side of the Los Angeles basin.

By noon the supermarket company posted a five-thousand-dollar reward for information leading to the arrest and conviction of the bandits.

Virgil Tibbs spent all the next day probing the background of Jerome Smith, the murder victim. He had had a juvenile record that began at age eleven, when he had been busted for smoking pot. At thirteen he had been arrested again for burglary and had been released in the custody of an aunt, his nearest known relative. Within six weeks he had been picked up again for the same offense and this time he had been sent to juvenile hall. In juvenile court he had been released on probation.

Four months after that he had been arrested, but rather than convict him of a felony the court had sent him to a home for boys in need of help and guidance. He was taken from there three weeks later for knifing another youth. He had then served six months in custody before being released.

The same sad, painful record went on, page after page. The maximum period that Jerome Smith had been out of trouble had been a little less than five months, and during that period he had been on parole. Around age sixteen he became a heroin addict and shortly thereafter was a known dealer. He was convicted of armed robbery while still a juvenile and the district attorney's petition to have him declared unfit to stand trial as a juvenile was denied for some reason. He served the better part of a year before again being paroled; during that time he had received medical attention as an addict and had been put on a methadone program.

Shortly after his release he was again arrested, this time for rape. His victim had been a fifteen-year-old black minister's daughter. When Jerome had pleaded for forgiveness and guidance, the minister had withdrawn the complaint and had stated that his daughter would not testify.

There were eight additional arrests before the incident involving Emily Myerson. His parents could not be located and his aunt had moved to an unknown address.

Tibbs conferred with several officers at the South Central Division of the Los Angeles Police Department. Then, in the company of a massive black sergeant, whom he recognized immediately to be a superior policeman, he visited the area where Jerome Smith had lived and hung out. He had had a single room, the walls of which were liberally covered with pornographic pictures.

He had had no steady girl friend. In the neighborhood he had had a reputation for having a violent temper. For that reason he had had few intimates. He had never held a job of any kind. His school records showed an adequate mind, but a total refusal to attempt to learn or to apply himself. He had been in trouble twice at school for molesting female classmates, but no formal action had been taken because of his age at the time.

The one thing Tibbs had hoped for—a possible known enemy or enemies—did not appear. Jerome Smith had been bad news and everyone else had apparently left it at that.

The black minister whose daughter he had raped, leaving her pregnant, had claimed the body and had given it a decent burial. He himself had conducted the service, at which only three others had been present. There had been no flowers or other tributes.

Tibbs went back to Pasadena in a grim frame of mind. For the first time in many days Miriam greeted him as though she did not have a cruel burden of her own to bear. She was pleasantly agreeable and had prepared a dinner so delicious that Virgil could not remember ever eating so well. The children were well behaved and he played with them for a few minutes before they were sent up to bed. Pierre gravely shook his hand and Annette gave him an affectionate kiss on the cheek.

In the morning Virgil laid out his cards once more on his desk and studied them for the better part of an hour. Since the first time he had done so, he had filled nine gaps in the original pattern. He made some changes, shifting data from one place to another, until at last he reached a definite conclusion. Bob Nakamura did not witness his effort, being out on a residential armed robbery that had gone down the night before and had been given priority.

Tibbs spent the rest of the working day checking into the background of Willis Raymond, the store clerk who had been pistol-whipped. There was no question of his having been a bona fide victim, but Tibbs knew how many cases had gone into the unsolved file because some minor lead had not been fully checked out. The attack on him had been vicious, so much so that it might have been premeditated. It was just possible that the store had been hit because Raymond worked there and someone had wanted him hurt.

Raymond had graduated from high school in the middle of his class. He had fought in Vietnam and had risen to the rank of sergeant in the Air Force before returning to civilian life. He had had a good record and had received an honorable discharge. He had had three traffic violations, none of them serious. Otherwise he had never been arrested. He had gotten along well with the customers in the store, where he had chosen to work the second shift because it paid a slightly higher salary. Some of his Negro customers thought that he was a racist, but Tibbs discounted that: There were blacks who considered every white American a racist. During his own visit with Raymond he had detected only a limited feeling, some of which had certainly been justified by his recent experience.

He was not intellectually very ambitious; he had a library card, but by the evidence in his room, he was not much of a reader. He had been born in Iowa and had come to California after his discharge from the military.

The revenge motive could also apply to his employer, and that fact took another full day of Tibbs's time. Rubin Goldfarb was married and the father of two children. He had indeed come into a considerable estate when he had turned twenty-five and he had made some prudent investments. He owned several motels as well as nine small retail grocery stores. He belonged to a health club where he worked out regularly. His credit standing was excellent. He had been born in Canada and was still a Canadian citizen. He had a reputation for being a ladies' man, which was not surprising in view of his physical appearance and financial resources. In the largest of his motels he kept one room permanently reserved for his personal use. He visited it approximately twice a week in the company of various young women, but this had never been the subject of any official notice.

He was an active sports fan and played an exceptionally

good game of tennis. He had had a year's training in karate at an inadequate school and had dropped out after sustaining an injury that was clearly the instructor's fault.

Only one thing turned up that was of interest to Tibbs: Goldfarb occasionally became aggressive; at such times he was inclined to push other people around in a manner that was sometimes strongly resented. He was aware of this problem and had sought professional advice in overcoming it. Probably as a result, the incidents in which he was involved materially dropped off. Unfortunately, Tibbs knew that some people held grudges for a very long time, particularly if their pride or vanity had been too severely wounded.

Virgil filled out a card on that and added it to his pack of carefully arranged facts.

Dr. William Pierce Smedley was fully entitled to his degree; he had earned it at an accredited college in the Midwest. Academically his field was American history. During the Vietnam conflict he had written a number of well-researched articles on the policy of no victory, which he had bitterly opposed. It had been his contention that if American boys were fighting, they should be allowed to attack all military targets and not be forced to ignore some for policy reasons. When that sad affair was over, he had objected to the amnesty offered to draft evaders and deserters who had fled to Canada and other havens. It had been his position that when so many had answered the call of their country and had given their lives, to excuse those who had taken what he called "the coward's way out" was morally unconscionable.

His personal life appeared to be above criticism. He had never been arrested. Although he drove a car, he had not had a traffic violation during the past three years, which was as far back as his computer printout went. He was not a member of any social or athletic clubs, devoting his full time to the organization he had founded to promote his particular brand of Americanism. Of special interest was the fact that he had never publicly encouraged any form of

112

violence. His was a "write to your congressman" style of campaigning.

His radio broadcasts, popular particularly in the Middle West, from which he had come, had a very wide audience, and requests for reprints were substantial. His organization operated almost entirely on donations. His life-style did not suggest that he was appropriating any of them for his personal use. Rather, he drew a remarkably modest salary and appeared to live entirely within that income.

Only one fact was significant: He was almost fanatically opposed to a parole system that released convicted felons long before their predetermined sentences had been served. He had given many talks on the subject, arguing that a fourth felony conviction should carry an automatic life sentence, as had once been the case in New York State. He also maintained that a citizen was entitled to take any action he considered necessary to protect his property and his home, including the setting of booby traps against possible invaders.

That, certainly, was an endorsement of violence in sharp contrast to his position on other matters. Tibbs filled out another card.

One other minor fact came to light only because Virgil was careful to check every angle. Arthur Myerson, Emily's father, was a staunch member of Dr. Smedley's political organization.

It was a few minutes past five when Tibbs's phone rang. Mrs. Stone was on the line with instructions from the chief; McGowan wanted him to remain in his office pending a further call.

That was unusual. Ordinarily he did not have a great deal of direct contact with the chief since the Pasadena Police Department was well organized and the channels of communication were clearly defined. He assumed at once that whatever the chief wanted, it was related to the Motamboru family. The most logical inference was that he was about to be relieved of that responsibility. In a way it would free him, but he knew deep within himself that that was not his dearest wish. The time would come, of course, when he would have to relinquish the company of Miriam and the children, but they had brought home to him very clearly something of what he had been missing.

But it went further than that. Miriam Motamboru was a rare and remarkable person. He had very little prospect of ever finding a girl like her on his own. She had unconsciously set a standard for him that was all but unattainable; it was fitting that her husband was a head of state because an ordinary policeman was not in a position to aspire to such heights.

He tried to ask himself if he was in love with her and then forced himself to block that thought from his mind. Every instinct told him that in that direction only disaster awaited him. He had been given an extraordinary trust; he would fulfill it no matter what the cost might be to him emotionally. Once before he had been interested in a girl, a nurse, but he had been a rookie then, with no assured future, and had not been able to compete with one of the doctors where she had worked.

As he looked back, it was just as well. If she had really been the girl for him, his status wouldn't have mattered. At least that was what he wanted to believe.

Miriam was a fine friend and the children were appealing. Also, her abilities as a cook certainly had enriched his life. But it would have to end. Mentally he tried to prepare himself for that as he waited for the chief's call.

He remembered to call Miriam and to tell her that he would be late. She promised to have something ready for him when he did get home.

It was not until after seven that his phone rang. He answered it quietly. It was McGowan, asking that Tibbs come up to his office. That was all.

Virgil put on his coat and straightened his tie as he walked toward the elevator. He knew then that he was fully prepared for whatever was to be asked of him. The family was not his; it had only been placed in his safekeeping for a brief, indefinite period.

As he rode up to the fourth floor, he allowed himself to

fantasize that someday he might be a guest at the presidential residence and have another of Miriam's fabulous meals. Only under those circumstances, certainly, she would not be doing her own cooking.

He stepped out on the fourth floor and went through the doors that led to the executive offices. They were all deserted except for the big suite on the left. He walked in and found the chief sitting with two other men he didn't know. He looked at them quickly and sensed with something close to certainty exactly who they were.

McGowan got up together with his two guests. "Gentlemen," he said. "This is Mr. Tibbs. Virgil, Mr. Reynolds and Mr. Conners. They are with the government."

That was a very open way of putting it: they could be from the FBI, the Secret Service, the CIA, or any other agency. Tibbs shook hands and joined the others when they sat down again.

Although the rest of the suite was empty, McGowan got up and closed the door. When he had seated himself again, he gave Tibbs a little more information. "Virgil, these gentlemen share the prime responsibility for Mrs. Motamboru and her children while they are guests in this country. It was their decision to bring them to Pasadena."

Tibbs nodded but did not interrupt.

"I think that Mr. Conners had better fill you in on what we've learned." McGowan settled back in his chair, indicating that he was for the moment withdrawing from the conversation.

Conners began. "Mr. Tibbs . . . Virgil, if you don't mind."

"Please."

"Bill. To start, Jim and I appreciate what you're doing to help us out. We have means of checking and we're pleased with the way you're handling things, particularly your relationship with Mrs. Motamboru. She's a damn attractive woman—we're aware of that."

Virgil said "thank you" only because it was expected of him.

"You know that President Motamboru is officially listed

as missing. He was in an untenable position vis-à-vis the guerilla attacks being made on his government and the military raids on the fringes of his country. So he was advised to get out. He refused, saying the usual thing about the captain staying aboard his sinking ship. But in a sense he was right; if he had pulled out, he couldn't have expected too much from the rest of his government."

"I agree with him," Tibbs said. "A cop doesn't give up his gun."

Conners glanced at his partner, who took over. "You might as well have it straight out, Virgil. He's dead. We have it on good authority. It's secondhand but reliable."

Tibbs sat very still. He knew what that news would do to Miriam, and he also sensed that he was going to be given the job of breaking it to her.

"How much room for error is there?" he asked.

"Damn little, if any. To be really honest with you—none. For God's sake don't tell her this, but he was in a small building with four of his aides. They burned it down. No one got out."

Conners took up the conversation once more. "We called on Mrs. Motamboru this afternoon. She told us—and these are her own words—that you have been the soul of consideration to her and her kids. We broke the news to her about her husband. We wouldn't saddle you with that one."

Virgil put his hands over his face. "She must be in agony," he said.

Conners suddenly became much more human. "I've made notifications before; this was one of the toughest. We've done some fast thinking. There's no place we could take her where she would be any safer than where she is now. Despite what's happened, she and her kids still need protection. She could rally a lot of support for what her husband stood for—and they know it."

"What you're saying is that they may look for her harder than ever."

"You've got it."

"You want me to continue as I have been?"

"Exactly."

"For how long?"

"Indefinitely, unless you want out."

Virgil looked at the chief. "I don't want out," he said, "but whether I continue or not isn't my decision."

McGowan looked at his two guests. "In that case, gentlemen, Virgil will stay on the job. And I'll tell you something else, officially. You're damn lucky to have him."

The air was getting a little too thick. Tibbs stood up and said, very calmly, "I think I'd better go home."

As he drove eastward, up Colorado Boulevard, he broke out in a cold sweat. He knew that from the moment he walked through the door of his temporary home the burdens on him would be twice what they had been before. And there were thoughts churning in the vortex of his mind that he did not dare let surface, no matter what the cost.

15

As he turned into the driveway, Virgil saw that the front door was open and that Miriam was standing just inside. He parked his car, got out, and tried his best to clamp an iron band on his emotions. If ever in his life he had had to keep himself under control, this was the time.

As he walked toward the door, the look he saw on Miriam's face did nothing to make his task easier. He saw her swallow hard and realized what a fearful thing it was that she had been called upon to face.

When she spoke to him, she kept her voice steady only with a determined effort. "I'm glad that you're home."

"I came as soon as I could." With that simple statement he told her that he knew. She could have assumed that, but he wanted her to be certain. He closed the door and turned toward her.

Before he could speak, she began again, almost mechanically. "I gave the children their dinner and sent them to bed. I didn't tell them. I thought that there would be time enough for that later. They aren't really prepared."

"I think you did the wise thing," Virgil said. "Give yourself some time first."

"Yes, I'm going to need that." She turned and began to walk away from him, but she only took a step or two before she stopped and faced him once more. "I have some dinner ready for you," she said.

"Have you eaten?" he asked.

"No, I didn't feel very much like it. Do you mind eating in the kitchen?"

They entered a very modern kitchen whose window provided a partial view of the city. He had planned to set the table in the breakfast alcove, but that had already been done. There were linen napkins in place and even a candle in the center of the small table. It would be the first time that they had ever eaten alone together.

She had a dish warming in the oven, something in a casserole. She set it out, sliced some French bread that had also been kept warm, and added a vegetable. She poured a sauce into a small serving dish. Virgil washed his hands and then sat down to eat. Miriam lighted the candle, a small symbol of the world she had known, and then seated herself across from him. Normally she used very little in the way of cosmetics; at that moment she wore none at all. She had combed her hair as she always did, but not with quite the same sense of chic; she had made herself presentable, but no more.

Tibbs waited while Miriam served him. She did this with all of her usual grace, and for that he admired her very much. Despite the fact that she was still in a state of shock, and grief-stricken, she had not lost one iota of her natural grace and manners. They had been so well developed in her that she could not have abandoned them if she had wanted to; to some degree they were now giving her moral support.

Virgil took his plate and thanked her. When he tasted the dish she had prepared, he had no idea what it was, but it almost melted in his mouth. For three or four minutes they ate quietly, communicating in the way that people can who understand each other and require no words to convey certain things.

When he felt that it was time, he broke the silence. "Miriam, I met two gentlemen from, I presume, the State Department in the chief's office this evening. They told me that they had called on you."

"Yes, they did," Miriam said. "It was very kind of them."

"I'm convinced that they have your welfare, and that of the children, as their first objective." He made it a simple, factual statement.

"I believe so too." Miriam looked at him and for the first time he caught a glimpse of the great pain she was experiencing just below the surface.

"In view of my . . . assignment, we discussed the matter. I hope that you don't mind."

She raised her dark eyes and looked into his. In that manner she assured him of her trust.

"They feel strongly that it would be very hazardous for you to appear publicly—anywhere—at the present time."

"I understand." She spoke so softly he could hardly hear her.

He decided to wait before going any further and turned his attention to the meal. Whatever the sauce was she had made for the vegetable, it added a tang that made it delicious. He had eaten in fine restaurants many times, but they had never served him anything comparable. When she had told him, at the outset, that she was a very good cook, she had stated the simple truth and no more.

He could not help comparing her as she had been then and as he saw her now across the table, fighting to hold herself together and doing a valiant job despite the fact that her composure was only due to extreme self-control. Then he reached out. "May I offer you my hand?" he asked.

She reached out and took it, first gently, then with increasing strength. She held on so tightly that he could feel her muscles quiver, and it came to him that this was their first real physical contact. It was far more binding than that one moment when he had so unexpectedly kissed her at her direction. That had been a business matter, a necessary piece of role playing. As he felt the pressure of her fingers, he received some of the pain that was in her and gave her some of his strength in return. He knew then that for the rest of his days he would have Miriam Motamboru engraved forever in his memory.

Somehow they finished the meal without talking anymore about the intolerable thing that had happened. When they were through, Virgil helped clear up; while Miriam put the food away, he stacked the dishes in the dishwasher—a convenience that was not one of the features of his own apartment. As he worked, he could not help feeling like an intruder, forcing himself on this woman whose grief had to be all-consuming. At the same time he knew that he was, in a way, supporting her—he was someone to talk to if she needed him for that. He could not go away and leave her, as they both knew, but he wished that he were not forced to be in such an awkward position. If he had been facing what she was, he would have wanted to be alone, very much alone.

The only solution was to take his cue from whatever indications she gave.

Miriam turned, looked around the kitchen, and satisfied herself that everything was in perfect order. As she moved into the living room, Virgil followed quietly behind her, prepared to say that he was going up to his room—but also ready to do whatever she wanted of him.

She sat down on the plush davenport, and looked up at him, silently inviting him to join her. He sat beside her, not too close but near enough to let her feel his presence.

She said nothing for what seemed a very long time; then she spoke less to him than to the otherwise empty room. "We have always known that something like this might happen, my husband and I, because Africa is a land of great promise and there are enormously greedy people in the world, people without morals and more ruthless than you can imagine."

She stopped. Virgil remained stone still.

"My husband gave his life for his country, I have that to console me. It never would have existed without him. He knew the risk and he took it. I wish that I could have been with him." Then, at last, she broke down in tears.

Virgil did not ask himself what he should do or what the department would expect of him under the circumstances. Instead, he reached out and offered himself in the hope that it would bring her some consolation. She put her head against his chest, overcoming her inhibitions and allowing her grief to burst its bonds. He handed her a large, clean handkerchief, put his arm across her shoulders, and held her so that she could feel some sense of security, some possible feeling that she was not suddenly all alone.

She cried until it was all out of her and she had no more to release. She was exhausted and began to breathe deeply against his shoulder.

In a few minutes she was fast asleep. It was a very awkward position for Tibbs; after a little while his muscles began to ache and he wondered how much longer he would be able to remain still. Then the discomfort eased and he was only aware of the sleeping woman next to him who was finding shelter in the forgetfulness of sleep.

It was sometime in the small hours of the night that she lifted her head and whispered very softly, "Are you awake?"

"Yes," Tibbs answered.

Somehow she understood everything, and he knew that she did. "Thank you," she said.

"Of course."

She roused herself and stood up a little unsteadily. "I want to go to bed; I should have gone long ago."

He escorted her up the stairs and to the door of her room. He left her there and then went silently to his own room. Minutes later he was asleep, getting what rest he could before he would have to face the unsolved problems that were impatiently waiting for the coming of early morning.

When he reached his desk in the morning, there was a startling new development. Bob Nakamura, who had come in even earlier than usual, filled him in. "It happened last evening. Some off-road riders had their bikes out in the desert just for the fun of it. They charged up a small hill and found something there. It scared the hell out of them, so they came right back and reported to the sheriff's station."

"A body?" Tibbs asked.

"No, a cache of arms that you wouldn't believe. All we've

got so far is that it's an arsenal, enough to equip a small army. Advanced stuff like automatic rifles, mortars. You name it."

"I'd better get up there," Tibbs said. "There are a few questions I'd like to ask whoever's in charge."

"The sheriffs are handling it; it's their jurisdiction."

Virgil thought. "There's a lot I've got to do, but this thing may make it unnecessary. If it's terrorists who planted that cache, it won't help me. But if it's superpatriots, then it may be a whole new ball game."

"Have you got a line on something, Virg?"

"Yes. It's pretty thin, although I'm confident of it. But there are too many gaps; there are at least two people I can't identify and I'm a long way from any kind of proof that will hold up in court."

"If you're going up there, I'd suggest that you call the Hall of Justice and get yourself set up. The bomb and arson people are handling it. Under the circumstances, they might appreciate knowing of your interest."

"Right," Tibbs agreed, and picked up his phone.

It was almost two hours later when he pulled up at a roadblock and identified himself. The deputy in charge at that point used his hand radio. When he had finished, he indicated the way up a barely visible dirt road. "Watch yourself," he advised. "We've found a lot more in the last hour and we don't know what the boundaries are."

"I'll be careful," Tibbs promised.

He drove down the desert track, going slowly and taking in everything that he could see. It was an almost totally primitive area, as was much of the vast desert. Thin track marks were the only evidence of human invasion. No power lines were visible and nothing whatever relieved the flat and empty vista that reached eastward literally for hundreds of miles. Among other things, it was an almost ideal place for the informal disposal of bodies; he had reason to believe that there were hundreds of human remains scattered across the wide terrain. Many had been found, but the vast majority lay undiscovered and probably would until Judgment Day.

After fifteen minutes or so he came to a cluster of official vehicles and pulled in and stopped. A uniformed sergeant from the sheriff's department intercepted him as he got out of his car. "What can we do for you?" he asked.

Tibbs displayed his badge. "What you've got here may tie in with a case I'm working on," he said.

"You'd better talk to the lieutenant, then. He's at the command post." The sergeant pointed toward a low hill. "That's where the stuff is. There's a helluva lot of it and some of it is pretty exotic. The bomb squad is checking it out; the rest of us stay down here below."

Tibbs thanked him and walked to the command post, where he was expected. He met Lieutenant Austin and again stated the purpose of his visit. As he did so, he noted two or three men in plain clothes in the immediate area; they, of course, would be FBI.

Austin took him to one side. "I can't tell you a great deal right now," he said. "This is one of the biggest caches of arms ever discovered in the States. There are rocket launchers, fully automatic weapons, and a lot of other stuff that has no business whatever in civilian hands or out in the desert like this, where anyone can find it—and someone did."

"Any indications as to the ownership?" Tibbs asked.

"Nothing definite yet, but absolutely off the record we think it may be a group that's been under surveillance for some time. They appear to think that the United States is about to collapse, so they plan to be ready to take over."

"How much stuff do they have here?"

"Say, a couple of million dollars' worth, taking into account the channels they had to use to get hold of these kinds of armaments."

"I've got two questions," Virgil said. "They may sound far out, but I'm dead serious."

"O.K. Go ahead."

"In addition to weapons, have you found anything, anything at all, that might be called execution equipment? Anything like a gallows or whatever?"

"Not to my knowledge," Austin answered. "Frankly, I

wouldn't expect anything like that. These characters would take care of things like that by standing somebody up against a wall and shooting him."

"Are there any ropes or things like that?"

"No, nothing like that so far." He used his handset radio. "Have you found any ropes or material of that kind?"

"Negative. We just uncovered some grenade launchers." "Ten four."

"There's your answer," Austin said. "So far it's strictly an arms cache; nothing more. But that's enough."

"Who's handling the IDing of the owners of this stuff?"

"The feds; you might talk to them."

Virgil had no trouble picking them out, but they weren't talking—even to a fellow officer. They couldn't honestly be blamed; they had a red-hot thing to handle and the less said publicly the better until some important questions had been answered. Three large trucks rolled in with Army personnel and markings. They would be munitions experts and would probably be taking some of the contraband equipment away.

As he drove back to Pasadena, Virgil realized that the long trip had probably not been worthwhile, but he had gained certain data and he would just have to be patient until the feds had established who had deposited the arms in the desert and for what purpose. When he was back in his office, he called several friends in various jurisdictions and asked for their help.

His best contact in the FBI was reasonably candid. "We're running it down, but it may take several days. A lot of people are involved. We've got a starting line, but nothing definite yet."

"Just tell me one thing," Virgil asked. "Is there a Pasadena angle? Because if there is, I may have something to contribute."

"As far as I know, Virg, there's nothing like that at the present time. I'll pass the word along that if a Pasadena lead does surface, they should get in touch with you immediately."

Tibbs thanked him and hung up. He knew that he would

have to wait while the feds did their work. Meanwhile, he went back to his own investigation. He spent most of the rest of the day in northwestern Pasadena, which was largely black, talking to a number of people he knew. His snitches were willing, but they couldn't give him a lead. Whatever was going on, the security was very tight.

He knew what he had to do next, but the task was staggering and the chances for a successful outcome were poor at best. But he had to attack it because he had no other way to go until he found out more about the weapons discovery in the desert. If that panned out, he would be in luck. It was a possible shortcut and he held his breath in anticipation of something from that find he could use.

Meanwhile, he went on with his meticulous checking of two different people who interested him very much.

Some very efficient work done by the sheriff's detectives in co-operation with the federal authorities having jurisdiction over tobacco, alcohol, and firearms turned up four of the people who had been responsible for the huge cache of weapons that had been stored in the desert. Within two days they had suspects in custody and under interrogation.

As the bizarre affair unfolded, there was little joy in it for Virgil Tibbs. Once caught, the weapons owners talked quite freely, but they also emphatically denied that they had had anything whatever to do with the two execution-type murders in Pasadena. Some alibi checking established that they were probably telling the truth. It wasn't a definitive answer since there were other suspects still to be taken into custody, but the outlook wasn't good.

At the end of a week, seven more had been apprehended and there still was no Pasadena connection. The possibility remained that there might be another arm of the group that was still under cover, but nothing that had been learned gave any credence to the idea. Every lead that Virgil had explored, no matter how fragile, had petered out and he found himself up against something close to a dead end.

He went to report to Lieutenant Smith, whose small office was located in the older part of the building. After refusing coffee, which was almost always brewing in the lieutenant's office, he confessed his position. "Dick, I'm right where I was a week ago on those two execution murders. I haven't got anything more to work on."

The lieutenant didn't question that. He knew Tibbs wouldn't admit defeat unless he was at a total dead end. "Have you got anything at all?" he asked.

"Yes," Virgil answered, "I have. I've got one solid fact that I don't think can be questioned. But there are at least two people involved that I haven't been able to make and I've tried everything in the book."

Smith remained relaxed, which was his usual style. "What chance have we got that a citizen may come forward—some break like that?"

Reluctantly Tibbs shook his head. "At this stage, practically none. The only thing that would help now would be another similar killing. If that were to happen, I'd certainly have more to work with. I can't say more than that."

Smith was a very astute man and he sensed immediately what was behind that remark. "Virg, if I read you correctly, you may know at least one of the people involved."

"I've got a pretty good idea," Tibbs answered, "but absolutely no proof. No evidence at all that I could use to justify an arrest. I'm up against an extremely resourceful and clever person who's in a very strong position and knows it. And everyone concerned has covered his tracks very well. That's about it," Tibbs confessed. "Of course, I may have overlooked something . . ."

"No," Smith interrupted, "I'm ready to assume that you haven't. That isn't your MO." He stopped and thought some more. "Let me ask you something," he continued. "Suppose, for the sake of discussion, you were to go and see the person you have in mind and inform him that you know about his activities. Would that stop any further executions?"

"It might, if I'm right."

"That makes the bottom line pretty clear, doesn't it? You may be able to stop more killings, but at the cost of letting a two-time murderer go free. Or you can let him go on

127

with what he's doing. If he kills again, then, knowing his identity, you could probably bust him with enough solid proof to stand up in court."

"That's just how I see it," Virgil replied. "Which is why I'm here."

"How about some kind of a stakeout?" Smith asked.

"It's almost impossible to set one up, even with heavy manpower. The only possibility is to wait until another known criminal, preferably a black one, is let loose and then keep him under close surveillance. For openers, the jurisdictional problems could be rough."

The lieutenant had to agree with that. There were so many different jurisdictions in Los Angeles County that this recurrent problem was one of the major headaches in law enforcement throughout the area.

He came to a decision. "I want to think this over for a little while, Virg," he said. "It's not something I want to call too fast."

Tibbs stood up to go. "Whatever you decide, Dick. But don't take too long; otherwise the matter may be taken out of our hands."

Although he had only been out on parole for less than five months, Willie Snodgrass was doing far better than he ever had before in his life. He was making money, lots of it, behind a cover so good that his parole officer had been favorably impressed.

He had learned a lot during his two times in prison. Not many people thought of Folsom as an acting school, but it was there he had learned so well how to play the role of a deprived young black man who had gotten into trouble only because of his environment and lack of opportunity. He also learned how to stammer out his heartfelt desire to make something of himself at last because crime was something he would never turn to again.

A good month before he had been released he had been offered a proposition. He had been looked over carefully by other inmates who knew his daring, his ruthlessness, and his hatred of anything to do with law and order. When he had been given the setup, he had gone for it immediately. As soon as he was on the outside, he had gone to Los Angeles and found a cheap room in the Watts area. Then he had called the number he'd been given, and asked for George.

The place was a large junkyard located not too far away from where he was staying. George talked to him only briefly. Willie was told to come in after a week's time. Obviously George was not one to say too much over the telephone, and that was good.

When Willie showed up exactly a week later, he was indignant that George was a white man. In a few seconds, however, he revised his opinion; George was hard, tough, and experienced, and he knew how to handle men. In any kind of a fight he would be deadly; he was as strong and as tough as anyone Willie had known in the joint.

George took him into a small, dirty office. "I hear from some friends of mine that you're a pretty good man, but I don't like it that you've been caught twice."

Willie scowled, but he had been told that George was as good as they came. "I ain't gonna get caught again," he said. "I'll kill every shithead cop first."

"I'll find out how good you are. Meanwhile, you go to work here as a yardman and you make it look good. If you don't, I'll can you. I never take any chances."

"How much do I get?" Willie asked.

"Minimum wage, what you'd expect coming right out of the slammer. But that's peanuts if you turn out to be the man I want."

Willie had never been formally employed before in his life, but he understood the importance of good cover. He did not overexert himself yet did enough actual work to convince his parole officer, when she called, that he was at last on the right track. He got a kick out of that because it was the right track all right, but not the one she thought.

Then George called him in again. "So far you look good," he said. "You're not afraid to get off your ass and get some dirt on your hands. You never know who's watching you and, like I told you, I never take any chances. Now, are you ready to make some real bread?"

"Damn right," Willie answered.

"Then tonight I'm going to try you out. There'll be three of us. The place has been cased good and I know the whole layout. But I want you to get this: we work as a team. And I mean a team; we each know what to do and how to do it. If you make one move on your own, you're out. Period. You shoot when you have to. If somebody doesn't do exactly as we say, and right when we say it, we hit 'em. Nobody gets brave with us. That suit you?"

"Just try me," Willie answered.

That night, together with another black man called Ty, they hit a small market. It was a rehearsal and Willie did just fine. When the owner slid his foot toward a possible hidden alarm, Willie smashed him behind the ear with his gun. It was simple after that. The whole take was less than a thousand dollars, but that didn't really matter.

Four days later they went all the way to Pasadena to make a hit and scored big. Willie again proved his ruthlessness and toughness and George seemed pleased. The next job was in Glendale and it went off with precision. The three of them were already a smoothly working team, each having complete confidence in the others.

When they got back to the junkyard, George held a council of war. "So far it's going good," he said. "It's gonna keep on going that way as long as you guys do exactly as I say, the way you have been. Next time we use a different car; I got dozens here that look like they're scrapped, but actually they run damn good. I see to that. And I've got all the license plates we need."

"What about my money?" Willie asked.

"That's another thing. A good way to get caught is to flash around a lot more cash than you're supposed to have. There's people who notice things like that. You get your share, but you bank with me. Whenever you want you can take it and split, but then you gotta go at least as far as Chicago so nobody can tie in what we take here with what

130

you spend. The longer you stick, the more you make."

Willie shut up because, hard as he was, he wasn't about to challenge George's bookkeeping. He was in on too good a thing.

"One thing more," George went on. "By now they've got us down as a white and two blacks and that's easy to spot. After each job we'll go to a spot I'll have picked in advance. There you let me off with the take, the guns, and the masks. Then you drive back here. If you get stopped, you haven't got a thing on you. I'll have somebody else pick me up, another guy with a different car. I'll have to pay him something, but it's worth it."

"You trust him?" Ty asked.

"He's my brother."

The next hit was at a market, a little more risky, but the take would be a lot more. It went fine. When one woman shopper disobeyed the order to freeze, Willie shot her in the shoulder and the rest was easy. Within four minutes after leaving the store, George was dropped off at a safe spot and Willie drove the car back to the yard. Nobody paid them any attention.

When George showed up they went over the take, which was unexpectedly big. Willie got more than four thousand dollars added to his pile, which almost doubled it. He was getting rich and he had never felt so safe in his life.

Miriam Motamboru took the call a little after five-thirty. She answered quietly, always careful not to reveal a thing until she was certain who the caller was. When she heard Tibbs's voice she relaxed, not for a moment forgetting that he was calling over an open line.

"I'll be a little late tonight," he advised. "An hour, maybe a little more."

"All right," she answered. When he hung up she knew that if anyone had been listening in, accidentally or otherwise, he had learned nothing. No names had been used and the call was far too brief to have been traced. The constant need for precaution was drummed into her and she respected it fully.

She only went to the market at certain prescribed hours. Frequently Virgil went with her, staying in the car until she came out again. He never went inside because if he met anyone whom he knew, there could be complications. It had already been agreed that if such a chance meeting did take place, her name would be Alice Simms and she would be a friend. That would be enough.

She did not need to do any heavy marketing, but she was unexpectedly low on milk for the children, and there were three or four other things that she needed. She glanced at the clock and saw that she was ten minutes into her designated shopping time. She was not sure if the store she used was covered during that special period, but her visits there had been completely routine. Because so many housewives were home preparing dinner for their families, she could shop quickly and efficiently.

She gathered up her purse, which contained three credit cards in the name of Alice Simms, and a few moments later backed the small car that she used out of the garage. She drove smoothly for four or five minutes, reached the market, and parked in a convenient space where the car could be seen if she were being covered by any agency. She went into the store and made her selections in less than ten minutes. When it was her turn, she paid in cash for her purchases and waited while they were being bagged.

When the checker suddenly stopped, Miriam turned and saw in one quick glance three powerful-looking men who had just burst in. They were wearing ski masks and they had guns in their hands.

"Freeze. Hands up!" one of them barked.

Miriam obeyed, instantly grateful for the false identification she carried in her purse. Thinking very fast, she decided that the men had not come for her. They quickly took up positions where they could command the entire store.

"Touch an alarm and you're dead!" the leader of the team snapped; he raised his gun to emphasize his words. Wearing the ski mask, he was a terrifying thing to behold, but

Miriam did not turn a hair. It was her immediate concern to be as inconspicuous as possible.

While the leader stood guard at the door, his gun aimed and ready, another masked man yanked the checker out of her slot so roughly that she fell to the floor. "Stay there," he commanded. He opened the cash register and began to scoop out the money. It was then that Miriam saw that he was black; she was sure that the leader was not. When her purse was snatched from her, she offered no resistance at all. She had been in acute danger before in her life and knew how to keep her head.

The black man who had emptied the register where she had just been checked out quickly jumped to the next one. She looked outside and saw that one of the white Pasadena Police patrol cars was entering the parking lot. She could not imagine how it had gotten there so fast, but she was so grateful to see it she almost wanted to cry.

"Bust!" the leader of the masked men yelled, and whirled to face the doorway at an angle. It was then that Miriam realized that he had taken a position just to one side of the entrance, where he could not be seen from the outside. With roof lights on, another unit appeared outside and Miriam knew that the robbers were going to be caught; somehow the alarm had been triggered. The thing she feared was being detained as a witness, and there was no way she could notify Tibbs to come and rescue her. Or was there? She could ask permission to call her husband and try to get him at his office or at home.

The second checker made a motion. The masked man closest to Miriam aimed and fired. In horror Miriam saw the girl jerk forward and then collapse. In a single leap the gunman grabbed Miriam from behind and rammed the muzzle of his gun hard against her head.

A sudden icy calm took hold of her and she knew that she was going to join her husband. In a flash she thought of her children and knew that Virgil would take care of them. She was ready for the bullet she knew she would never feel. Then she was violently pushed toward the entrance while the man behind her kept his gun pressed hard against her skull.

She heard a scream and knew that the checker who had served her had been snatched up and was being used as a shield by the second man. Without moving her head, she could see that the police were not coming in; they were waiting for the robbers to come out.

She was pushed forward again until the door in front of her opened automatically. Then she heard the white leader shout from behind her, "Get out of the way! Back off or they get it right now!"

The checker was close enough for her to hear the girl's frantic breathing; she had to be terrified out of her wits. The leader was close behind them and she could almost feel his rage. Then he shouted once more, "We're walking out of here. Anyone who tries to stop us is dead. And we'll kill the women."

The checker screamed, but she was utterly helpless. Miriam knew that she was defenseless herself: The bandit holding her had his left arm under hers and his hand across her breasts. That made it impossible for her to drop down and expose her captor to police fire. Also, if she did that the checker would die; she had no doubt of that whatever.

The man holding her pushed her forward once more. Police guns were leveled, but wisely no one fired. Then she found herself next to an old and dirty car. Her captor opened the rear door and slid inside, still holding her and forcing her onto his lap. The swooning checker was taken into the front seat the same way. Not for a moment were the guns taken from either of their heads.

The gang leader crouched and opened the driver's door. "If any car moves off this lot or tries to follow us, we'll kill one and throw the body out. If you don't believe me, look inside."

Switching his gun to his left hand, he aimed it at a heavily built woman who had come close so as not to miss the excitement. She froze in sudden terror. He twisted the key to start the engine and was out of the parking lot in seconds.

The patrol car that had first come on the scene had been making a routine check; the second unit had seen it stop and had rolled in to investigate. At that moment the hostage situation had gone down and it had been impossible to use the radio. The moment that it was, Officer Jarado Blue put out a 211, reported hostages taken, and asked for the helicopter. When his partner ran up with news of the casualty, he reported it and asked for paramedics code three.

Communications came back at once for a detailed description of the suspects and their vehicle. Officer Blue reported that it was a salt-and-pepper team wearing ski masks. The car was an old Chevrolet or Plymouth, neutral color, license unknown at that moment. Full attention had been concentrated on the hostage situation and the license plate had been bent up underneath in the rear.

Almost before he finished speaking, the duty helicopter was in the air and headed for the location. Throughout the city patrol units were flashed the message. The field supervisor rolled code two to the scene with two more backup units. The paramedic van arrived at the same time that he did.

Very fast reporting by the officers who had been on the scene revealed that one of them had been at an angle where he could partially read the license plate. He had two figures and one letter that appeared to have been tape modified.

The field supervisor knew that the suspects were totally vicious and that, as of that moment, the outlook for their hostages was poor at best.

Radio calls blanketed the area and notified all nearby jurisdictions, but ten minutes after the robbery had gone down, the getaway car had apparently vanished from sight.

16

Virgil Tibbs drove home calmly, the police radio in his car turned off. It was there for emergency use only and he was not expected to have it on during his free time. Whenever he was needed, he could usually be located by phone in minimum time.

He pulled into the driveway, parked, and went to the front door. Quite often Miriam was there to meet him, but he was late and she was most likely busy in the kitchen giving the children their dinner. He opened the door with his key and found Pierre standing just inside.

"Hello," Tibbs said. "Were you waiting for me?"

"I thought it was my mother," the boy answered. His English was a little better, but his accent was still strong.

All of Virgil's faculties were alerted in a flash. "Did she go out?" he asked, remembering to keep his words simple.

"Yes, sir, to get some things for dinner."

"How long ago?"

Pierre pondered. "It is twenty minutes, I think."

The time was reasonable, but Tibbs was not entirely satisfied. "I'll go and get her," he said. "Keep the door locked until we come back."

"Yes, sir."

Virgil got back into his car and drove toward the supermarket where Miriam always did her shopping. There was only one convenient route, so he watched carefully, expecting to meet her coming in the other direction. When he reached the parking lot and saw the official vehicles, a sudden cold terror seized him. He drove rapidly across the bare asphalt and pulled up almost directly in front of the doors.

A young patrolman he did not know immediately came to the driver's window of his car, but before he could speak Virgil had his badge out. The youthful officer took a quick look and his attitude changed at once. "What went down?" Tibbs asked.

"The market was hit with a two eleven a few minutes ago. Three men in ski masks; we think it was the salt-and-pepper team we've been looking for. It was bad. They shot a cashier and she's probably in S-4 condition. And they took two hostages."

"Why hostages?" Tibbs almost barked.

The patrolman was surprised by his tone but answered promptly. "My partner and I rolled past, just to check that everything was all right. We saw the bandits, but before I could call for backup, another unit apparently saw us and rolled in. We knew the silent alarm would have been hit, so we took up positions to nail them as they came out."

"And then?" Virgil was almost boiling inside.

"Shots were fired. They hit a cashier and she went down. Then one of them grabbed the other cashier as a hostage. They also took a customer."

"Did you see all this?"

"Most of it. When they came out with the hostages, we followed the book to protect their lives."

Virgil forced himself to keep his voice calm. "Describe the other hostage to me."

"A female, black, about thirty-five, medium build, slender, five feet four or five."

"Was she attractive?"

"She had a scarf over her head, but I'd say yes. Very much a lady."

That did it. For a few seconds Tibbs could hardly control himself. Then he got out of his car and spoke briefly with the field commander, whom he knew well. That erased the last doubt. He wanted desperately to take immediate action, but he had another duty first. He went into the market, dropped a dime into a telephone, and called McGowan's private number.

When the chief answered, Virgil was concise. "I got home just a few minutes ago. My subject had gone to the grocery store, unescorted as far as I know. While she was there, it was hit by the salt-and-pepper team. Shots were fired and two hostages were taken, a cashier and my subject. Following hostage-situation rules, they were allowed to escape from the parking lot. That's all I've got."

McGowan thought very fast. "Was it a two eleven or were they after her?"

"A two eleven surprised by a cruising unit." Then he broke. "For God's sake, let me do something!"

"Have you got a radio car?"

"No."

"Take one and keep in touch."

Virgil ran out of the store and almost knocked down the field supervisor in his anxiety. "I need a car," he demanded. "Fast!"

The sergeant had never seen Tibbs blow his cool like that before and couldn't understand it, but he pointed to an unmarked detective unit close by. If Virgil was in that much of a hurry, there had to be a damn good reason.

Tibbs jumped into the car and turned up the radio. Traffic was normal until he switched to channel two and discovered that it was being used for the hostage situation. He had a desperate, almost irrational, urge to drive somewhere, anywhere, in search of the getaway car, but as yet he had no description, no license—nothing at all to go on.

As he listened to the communications, he forced himself to put his emotional involvement aside and to revert to the rigorous training that was so much a part of his life. He had spent years studying Aikido, probably the most advanced of the martial arts, and he knew how to keep his one point—to maintain possession of himself despite any possible outside influences.

Ben Hetherington came up to the window. "Care to fill me in, Virg?" he asked.

"The black lady taken hostage happens to be a very good friend of mine."

"I'd heard that you'd moved, Virg. Off the record, I thought you might have taken a roommate."

"Something like that, Ben. But hold it."

"Of course. Right now we're at a standstill. This is my car. Why don't I drive you back to the station where you can pick up one of your own. We'll keep in touch and if anything at all turns up we'll go after it together."

"Sold," Tibbs said, and slid over on the seat. Then he remembered something he should have thought of much sooner. He picked up the radio microphone and switched to channel one. He hated to turn off two, but it had to be done. "Tibbs," he said. "I want a meet with Nakamura. Urgent."

"Tibbs, stand by."

As Ben drove smoothly off the lot and headed westward, each passing second was agony for Virgil. Then he got his response.

"Nakamura is code five in the northeast area."

Of course. Tibbs suddenly understood. As soon as the chief knew that Miriam had been taken hostage, he would have notified Nakamura to cover the house. Bob was the only other member of the department who knew about Miriam Motamboru and her children. Code five meant stakeout, which was enough.

Back on channel two, the radio traffic continued, but the incoming reports were all negative. Four possible suspect cars had been stopped, cleared, and then thanked for co-operating. Nothing whatever on the airwaves indicated that one of the hostages was a VIP. By that time the federal people would have been notified of the situation; they would take whatever additional action they considered advisable.

By the time they reached the parking lot behind the police building, nothing new or encouraging had come in. Together with Ben, Virgil went inside to consult with the watch commander and check out a vehicle of his own. He also took a handset radio and a second small weapon that he kept on hand for emergencies. It was a two-shot derringer that he could conceal with a clip on his left hip so that it was almost invisible, even with his coat off. It carried magnum rounds and, despite its tiny size, was a lethal tool if he had need of it.

He called the house and was doubly reassured when Bob Nakamura answered the phone. Bob had a scanner with him and was following the radio traffic. There was nothing Virgil could do now but wait.

As Willie Snodgrass sat in the back of the car, the black woman on his lap and his gun pressed against her side, he was in a state of raw nerves. He hoped that George would get them out of it somehow. The frightful image of prison was projected in his brain; if he were caught this time, it would be years and years before he would get out again.

George took another turn and they were out of the residential area, where there were too many eyes. After half a block he turned down an alley, drove a few seconds more, and swung into an open garage, one apparently used for medium-sized trucks. As soon as he had cleared the opening, a man inside pushed a button and the door slowly closed.

"Out!" George commanded. Willie and Ty got out with their hostages. Neither of the women offered any resistance. The fourth man, who had been waiting in the garage, understood the situation immediately. He whipped out a gun and backed Miriam and the cashier into a corner, holding them there.

The well-rehearsed drill was gone through again, exactly as it had been each time the gang had operated. Without wasting a second, George gathered the loot and the ski masks into a canvas sack. A plain black Buick that looked like a well-maintained private car was waiting, its trunk already open. He threw the sack into the back, along with three of the guns. As he did so, Willie and Ty began to switch the license plates on the getaway car. The new set matched the type of vehicle in case any prowl car was suspicious enough to run the number. The old plates were stashed in the trunk of the Buick so that the car used for the hit was clean.

Willie and Ty would drive it back to the junkyard. It had been chosen because of its inconspicuous appearance; if it were to be stopped because it resembled the getaway car, it was completely clean and the new plates would check out; there was no way it could be held. George and his brother would drive the Buick. That was also safe because there was no description of it whatever and it would be driven by two white men. It would look completely respectable and the plates George had fitted also matched the vehicle. The car the plates really belonged to had been wrecked and was kept, unreported, in the back of the junkyard, free of wants or warrants. The police would be looking for one white man and two blacks; after the switch, that combination wouldn't exist.

As an additional precaution, the two cars always returned to the junkyard by different routes. The same rendezvous and exchange point was never used twice.

But the police had never been so close behind and, together with the added complication of hostages, something else would have to be done very fast. Every minute that went by meant that more and more patrol and detective units would be swarming the streets and covering all of the freeway entrances. It was a desperate situation, but George had been in tight corners before. An immediate decision was essential. George glanced once at the hostages and made it.

It would have required a maximum effort to attempt to seal off a city the size of Pasadena located in the midst of a huge metropolitan area. A complete blockade was virtually impossible, but it was still very nearly accomplished. All regular calls for police service were closely screened; those dealing with barking dogs, loud music, and similar 415 complaints were deferred. Two assigned patrol units handled all the rest as best they could. Everything else that the Pasadena Police Department could muster—every patrol unit, unmarked car, and three-wheeler that could be utilized as a police vehicle was pressed into service.

The reservists were called in, plus every off-duty regular officer who could be located. On request from the watch commander, the sheriff's department rolled the Special Enforcement Bureau black and white units to augment the Pasadena cars. All nearby jurisdictions were alerted. They were willing to help, but they had a steady flow of their own problems.

The stable doors were locked as well as could be done—this despite the fact that the horse had probably already been stolen. The whole operation was activated with all possible speed, because every minute that was saved increased the chance of success. As many units as could be mustered patrolled the streets, looking for the gray car or any vehicle that might be part of the operation. Kidnapping being a federal offense, the FBI was also alerted. Overhead, the duty helicopter remained airborne and ready for immediate action.

Several hundred motorists wondered what was going on and a number asked. They were politely told to move on. In the car assigned to him, Virgil Tibbs wove his way up one street and down another, putting himself, as far as possible, in the bandits' place and trying to visualize what they might do. He kept his eyes on the road and on everything else in his field of vision, listening intently to every word that came over the radio.

In every major police investigation a great deal of effort and work goes on that remains virtually unknown to the public. Every point of attack that might apply to a given situation is utilized. The National Crime Information Center holds a vast amount of information in its computers concerning methods of operation, physical descriptions, outstanding warrants in jurisdictions throughout the country, and other data. Reverse directories, voter registration lists, motor vehicle registrations, firearms ownership records, and moniker files all yield facts that may contribute to a case profile.

Witness interviews are much more thorough than is generally believed. Witnesses often see or note something that to them is of no importance but that may contain a vital clue needed to bridge the gap between one set of known facts and another. The tens of thousands of questions asked are all to a purpose and the answers received are very carefully noted. This thoroughness is illustrated by a famous case handled by the FBI. With only a slight written clue to go on, agents examined more than three million public documents until a handwriting match was finally found. When it was, an urgently wanted criminal was put behind bars.

A great deal of work had gone into the case of the salt-and-pepper team. From that effort certain facts had emerged. For one thing, it had been determined that after each of the known robberies absolutely no one could be found who had seen one white man and two blacks riding in the same car anywhere in the vicinity of each incident.

The California Highway Patrol had once stopped a car answering the general description of the getaway vehicle not long after the hit in Glendale. The vehicle had contained two Caucasian males who had been cooperative and the license plate had come back as clean, with no wants or warrants. There had been no justification for any further action because the eyewitness descriptions of the wanted car had been vague as to make, model, year, and color. It had been variously described as gray, tan, pale blue, and brown. Had the driver shown the least inclination to flee, or taken any other suspicious action, police reaction would have been immediate.

Some very meager facts had come from various eyewitness accounts. They offered no workable leads, but they were all dutifully recorded and circulated to the detective teams working on the case. One item was that two different witnesses who had not seen the actual holdup but had been several blocks away had noted an impressive black car parked where such a vehicle was not normally seen. One of the witnesses was almost sure that it was one of the smaller-sized Cadillacs; the other wasn't sure but thought that it might be a Buick.

Officer Jeff Cantrell sat alone in his patrol unit in the normally quiet sector of Pasadena, south of Colorado Boulevard and down toward San Marino and the famous Huntington Library. It was an area of luxury homes where disturbances seldom occurred, but where the temptation for burglars was considerable. Consequently, Officer Cantrell kept alert to note anything in the way of an unusual occurrence or anyone on foot who didn't appear to belong in the vicinity.

Officer Cantrell was also listening intently to his radio; he was aware that the salt-and-pepper team had hit again and that this time hostages had been taken. He assumed that the bandits had made a car switch, so any vehicle could be suspect. While most routes out of Pasadena were via main surface streets and freeways, there were two or three ways to leave the city by driving through the quiet sector where Officer Cantrell was on patrol. He knew that he had almost nothing to go on, but he had developed a policeman's instinct for seeing and noting the unusual.

When the black Buick sedan came down one of the crosstown streets, he paid it no particular attention; the driver was behaving properly and he hadn't been informed of the tiny piece of evidence possibly involving this type of car. Then, just ahead of him, the Buick turned a corner.

There was absolutely nothing outwardly wrong with that, but to Cantrell's expert eye the *way* that the turn had been made had been just slightly unusual. Normally a driver who knew that a patrol car was half a block behind him would be expected to show the usual symptoms of black and white fever: the unusual decorum of drivers who know that the watchful eye of The Man is on them. The Buick had cut the corner just a little short and a trifle faster than might have been expected.

There were millions of drivers in the Los Angeles area, but there were well-established patterns ranging from two middle-aged women constantly talking in the front seat to the unmistakable deuce—the drunk driver. Officer Cantrell had been on the force eight years and he pretty well knew them all. He sensed that the Buick was in something of a hurry, which was normal, but there was also a suggestion that the driver was trying to conceal it. That, too, was to be expected in the presence of a police vehicle, but in Cantrell's judgment the driver of the Buick wasn't trying to conceal it quite enough. It was a very tenuous suspicion, but enough to interest him.

He picked up his microphone and ran the license number. It came back in order: a black Buick registered in Pomona—no wants or warrants.

Still, having nothing else to engage his attention at the moment, Cantrell waited to see what the driver would do next. He followed the car at a safe distance.

The Buick turned another corner, this time even a slight bit faster. Everything was still perfectly proper, but to Cantrell the second change in direction did not logically follow from the first. The driver could be slightly lost, but if he were, he would be slowing down to read the street signs.

Officer Cantrell did not follow the Buick. Instead, he went straight ahead and turned at the next corner. He added a little speed to his patrol pace to give himself an advantage. When, after three short blocks, the Buick suddenly crossed in front of him, he considered that it qualified as a suspicious vehicle. And the Pasadena Police were urgently searching for any and all kinds of suspicious vehicles.

Officer Cantrell used his head. Instead of falling in behind the Buick, he radioed the Buick's location and direction and deliberately drove away from it at right angles.

The airborne Pasadena helicopter had the information within seconds. The pilot banked sharply, took up a new heading, and gave a two-minute ETA.

Four blocks away Sergeant Terry Blumenthal was in a command unit. He immediately took up a heading to intercept the Buick and keep it under observation.

But the Buick made still another turn, this one southward toward the edge of the city. No one spotted it, but Blumenthal was lucky; he saw the car coming right at him. He waited until it had passed and then reported its new position and direction. A prompt query went out to the

Pomona Police to ask if the registered owner of the Buick was known to them.

Running code two, Virgil Tibbs joined in the pursuit as fast and as safely as he could without either lights or siren. When Terry Blumenthal reported the car's most recent position, Tibbs was only a block and a half away. Seconds later he spotted the car. When he saw it again turn a corner, all doubt was erased: The driver did not want to be interviewed by the police.

Cantrell and Blumenthal had both reported that the car held two male occupants. Terry, who had had the advantage of a head-on view, added that they were middle-aged Caucasians. Neither report excluded the possibility of another passenger on the floor of the rear seat or even in the trunk.

The helicopter advised that it had the suspect vehicle in sight. Although there was still nothing to go on but the gut instinct of Officer Cantrell and the subsequent maneuvers of the driver, four Pasadena units began to run a perimeter around the Buick, aided and supported by four of the sheriff's SEB cars. The sheriff's department did not commonly use the term SWAT, but that was the SEB's function; the men manning the special units were qualified to deal with any situation that might develop. It was already a case of armed robbery, kidnapping, and possible murder, which was about as heavy as it could get.

When all of the units were positioned, the decision was made to stop the suspect vehicle. There had not been any real traffic violation on which to base a charge, but no one wanted to see a high-speed pursuit or a shots-fired situation develop if either could be avoided. If the occupants of the Buick were good citizens, they would cooperate and would be thanked for their assistance. It would be a disappointment, but there were a great many of those in every facet of police work.

Sergeant Blumenthal, visibly backed by another unit, pulled behind the Buick and turned on his roof lights. Since he was alone in his unit, he exercised maximum caution without giving away the fact that he was anything other than routinely composed. He put on his hat in preparation for getting out. When the Buick obediently stopped, he pulled his patrol unit six feet behind it with a thirty-inch overlap so that the left side of the patrol car would protect him as he stood in the street. The backup unit stopped across the street, where the two officers in it could keep the scene constantly in view. Out of sight four more cars were waiting, engines running, where they could be on hand in seconds if needed.

The driver of the Buick got out and stood in the street as Terry Blumenthal approached him. "What's the matter, officer?" he asked. "Did I miss a stop sign?"

Blumenthal saw the possible trap almost instantly and avoided it.

"No, sir, there wasn't any stop sign. But there was a pedestrian who had stepped off the curb about four blocks back. You failed to yield the right of way."

"I'm sorry, officer, but I didn't see any pedestrian at all," the driver said quite truthfully. "Was he in plain sight?"

"No," Terry answered. "He was in the shade under a tree where you could have missed him. But may I see your driver's license anyway, please?"

The driver relaxed. He sensed immediately that after an admission like that, the officer could not issue a citation. His driver's license would be looked at and then he would be let go with a warning. Furthermore, the cop was probably bored and had stopped him just to break the monotony of an eight-hour patrol.

Terry glanced in the rear seat of the Buick, making sure that no one was hidden on the floor. Then he stepped behind the black car and examined the driver's license. The small card with the color photograph was in order, but the name and address did not correspond with the registered owner.

He carefully handed the license back and assumed a more casual tone. "In view of the fact that the pedestrian was, to some degree, hard to see, I'm going to call it a warning this time."

"Thank you very much, officer," the driver said.

"While you are parked," Terry continued, "I'll give your

car a quick field safety check. You can get back behind the wheel."

In response to Blumenthal's directions, the driver obligingly demonstrated both beams of his driving lights, ran the windshield wipers, and briefly sounded his horn. He began to display signs of impatience, but he was intelligent enough to try to keep them suppressed.

"Fine," Blumenthal said. "Let me see your spare tire and you're on your way."

"It's in the trunk."

"I expect that it would be."

"Wait a minute, officer. I forgot. It's out for repair. My wife had a flat and left the tire at a filling station."

"It only takes a very few minutes to plug a tire, sir. I'm sure it's back where it belongs."

The driver shook his head. "I'm positive that it isn't there. If it's an infraction to drive without a spare, I'm sorry."

"I suggest that we look in the trunk anyway." Terry said. He stepped a little to one side, just in case the driver of the Buick decided to attempt something foolish. The driver leaned out and said, "I'm sorry, officer, but I'm terribly late. Thank you for your help."

His engine was already running, so he covered almost a full block before two of the sheriff's SEB cars stopped him again. This time the two occupants of the Buick found themselves surrounded by four large, capable-looking deputies, two of whom were carrying shotguns. "Get out of the car, mister," one sergeant ordered. "Keep your hands in plain sight. We'd like to have a look in your trunk."

George played his final card. He put his hands up against the windshield of his car, but he did not get out. "There's two hostages," he said. "Two women. You'll never find them and they'll be dead in an hour if I don't call a certain number and pass the word that I'm all right. If you want them to live, just step back and we'll be on our way. And get that goddamned helicopter off our tail. Can you understand me, copper?"

The SEB deputy had his gun in his hand in a flash and

pressed the muzzle firmly against George's head. "You've got five seconds to get out of that car," he said, "and to spread yourself flat on your belly on the street, arms above your head, legs apart. Do it *now*!"

George was desperate, but the gun was cold and hard against his skull. Two shotguns were trained, one on his partner, the other on himself. He had no choice whatever. As he got out of the car and stretched himself prone, he remembered that he knew a smart lawyer. Illegal search and seizure might be a good place to begin. Cops could be tough, but the courts were sometimes too lenient to be believed.

17

Virgil Tibbs had not lingered at the scene. He had been parked just around the corner in case more manpower was needed, but when the word was flashed on the special frequency that the two suspects were in custody, he knew that his presence would not be required. The SEB cars would be able to handle anything that went down if the party got rough—and he had urgent business elsewhere.

He reasoned rapidly and carefully. A car change had been all but inevitable, but there was still the original getaway car and no vehicle even remotely like it had been spotted trying to get out of the city. Therefore there was a good chance that it was still in Pasadena. It could have been abandoned in favor of a third vehicle, but it was more likely that the two black bandits would try to use it to escape when they felt they had a chance. Meanwhile, they still held their two hostages somewhere, and they might well try to use them to buy their freedom.

Four minutes later he learned, by radio, that the two white suspects were good for the job and that one of them had tried to bargain the hostages for a pass out of the city. That meant there were four men in the team: three to pull the jobs and the last to drive the Buick and help with the car switch. Since the Buick would be the less suspicious vehicle, it would be used to carry the loot.

Very shortly he had confirmation of that. The trunk of the Buick had contained the loot, the ski masks, and two guns. Both of the suspects in custody had been armed, but when faced with the SEB shotguns, they had taken the only way out they could, discounting suicide. They were pros, and a pro knows when to give up. There are always lawyers and frequently bail. A lot of money was carefully hidden at the junkyard, and the Mexican border was relatively close by.

Although he already knew the answer, Virgil put out a call to ask if there was any further information concerning the hostages. There wasn't. If anything had been learned, it would have been put on the air in seconds.

He used the brain with which God had blessed him and headed his car toward the northwestern sector of Pasadena—the predominantly black area. Most of the residents would recognize the unmarked unit he was driving as a police vehicle, but the men he was after almost certainly weren't Pasadena residents. They had to be in a bad situation: their two Caucasian partners had apparently left them with the hostages, who should have been let go a few minutes after the robbery. But hostages could talk and would have descriptions to give. There was another alternative, but even the subconscious awareness of it filled Tibbs with a cold and paralyzing fear.

Just north of Pasadena there were mountains rich with canyons and gullies that were genuine wilderness areas. Fire roads led in and out of that forbidding terrain. In the past, many bodies had been recovered in that region and many more undoubtedly lay undiscovered. It was a possible way out if they wanted to be sure that their hostages kept silent.

Virgil forced his mind back to the immediate task at hand. In the black community the two bandits still at large would be less distinguishable; they might even have arranged for a place to hide until the first heat was off. Virgil called in a code six, indicating that he was leaving his vehicle to investigate, and sought the help of a well-known black prostitute who missed almost nothing that went on. She was willing to talk to him, but she had no news to give. Three other quick contacts confirmed what she had told him: No one in the regular community knew anything.

151

He believed them because he had had the case tabbed as an outside job from the beginning.

He went back to his car, knowing that the helicopters were busy checking all of the mountain fire roads with infrared detectors but realizing that sooner or later the near blockade of the city would have to be lifted. The cost in manpower was staggering and the city still had to be policed, particularly after dark. Every burglar in the trade would know that almost all of the police facilities were concentrated at the freeway ramps and outgoing surface streets, so the pressure to have policemen return to their normal duties would be constantly mounting.

With all the self-discipline that he could muster, he forced from his immediate thoughts the knowledge that they held Miriam. His best hope in aiding her rescue, if it were possible, would be to use his skills and his training and to function as a member of the team as soon as anyone struck any kind of a lead. The captured bandits would be under intense interrogation—probably by Sergeant Ott, an expert at that sort of thing—but they would be pros and therefore would probably be tight-mouthed.

He pulled his car over to the curb in a residential area and just sat for a few minutes, putting himself in the place of the bandits and analyzing exactly what he would do. When he had thought that out, he began a systematic patrol up and down the streets and alleys of the northwest sector of the city. He knew just what he was looking for and where he expected to find it. He drove slowly, casually, as though he were looking for a chance to pick up a girl. He debated taking his unit down and trading it in for a true undercover car, but he couldn't take the time: He decided to stay with what he had.

His decision firm in his mind, he turned down another obscure alley. Pulled over to one side was an old Ford of nondescript color. There was a black man sitting behind the wheel.

Tibbs had the window down already; he pulled up casually beside the car and leaned out.

"Hey, brothah," he said in the thick, unmistakable drawl

152

of the Deep South. "Wheh cun ah get mahself a woman 'round heah?"

The moment he had seen the plain tan car turning into the all but unused alley, Willie Snodgrass was instantly alert, a gun hidden under his right leg. He was not going back to prison, no way, no matter what he had to do to avoid it. His trained eye told him that the plain car was just a little too respectable; it could even be a cop car.

When it pulled alongside he was ready to shoot to kill, but the voice calmed him down somewhat. No northern cop talked like that, or could, and the fact that the man who had spoken to him was dressed up meant that he was looking for a classy lay; none of the streetcorner girls would do for him.

But he was still suspicious. He listened acutely for the giveaway sound of a police radio. Virgil had thought of that and had snapped it off so that not even a pilot light showed.

Then Willie saw a possible way out. The stranger wanted to break the law. Maybe providence had sent him to help Willie out of a terrible jam. "If you wanna talk to me, you come ovah here," he said.

Virgil got out of the car. Willie watched him intently, noting that although he was well dressed, he kept his head thrust out a little. The license plate of his car had been changed, but the vehicle itself could be identified as suspect. Too many people could have had a good look at it in the supermarket parking lot—and some of them had been cops.

Tibbs fearlessly walked up to the side of Willie's car, his movements reflecting his origin in the black ghettos of the South. He acted as if he were high on something, maybe grass; he would therefore be more pliable. "Brothah," he said. "You looks like a man who kin help me. I got mahself some good bread. Now I wanna real high-class woman. You got anybody?"

Instantly Willie knew that he had been spotted as a pimp. It would explain his being where he was, out of sight, and the scanner radio that was in the open glove compartment of his car.

153

"Mebbe," Willie said, "but I don' know you, brothah, not at all."

Tibbs put some hardness into his voice. "Listen, friend, you don' have to know me. Fact, ah don' wan' you to. Anybody ask you, you nevah seen me—nobody like me. Ah ain' nevah been heah."

"You done time?" Willie asked.

Tibbs sneered. "Naw, man, and ah ain' gonna. They don' know me and there ain' no way they'se gonna find out. 'Cause when ah'm through, ah moves on, 'fo anybody knows anythin'. You dig, brothah?"

It fitted. Willie kept the smirk off his face, but he knew a rank amateur when he saw one. He could use his car, his bread and, what was more, there wouldn't be any squawks to the cops—he couldn't afford it.

He pocketed his gun and said, "Let's go ovah to youah ca'." Prison had taught him a great deal and he knew how to deal with amateurs. He was lightning fast with his gun and he was considerably bigger than this man.

He swaggered slightly over to Virgil's car and looked inside through the passenger's window. When he saw the police radio, he instantly tried to jump aside and whip out his gun, but he felt the hard pressure of cold steel against the small of his back and then the unmistakable click as the hammer was drawn back. He realized that if he were shot where he felt Tibbs's gun, he might survive, but he would probably be paralyzed for life.

"Assume the position," Tibbs said in his normal voice. "You're under arrest on suspicion of pandering."

Willie felt the gun being lifted from his own pocket before he expected it and was at once at a great disadvantage. He had been suckered in, something that never would have happened if he hadn't been so concerned with the need to escape.

They couldn't make a charge of pandering stick—he was sure of that—but if he were in jail overnight and then released, he might be better off than he was. They would search his car, but there was nothing whatever in it to tie it in with the burglary.

Also, he had by no means made up his mind that he was going to go quietly. He had carefully noted that Tibbs had not called for backup, so maybe he wasn't so smart either. Tibbs was black, only the two of them knew that an arrest was being made so there was a good chance of a deal. Cops had been bought before; in fact, there was a good chance he had been busted just so a deal could be made. And what the hell was Pasadena but an overgrown hick town!

Tibbs cuffed him expertly even though he didn't have a partner or any backup; Willie knew then that this was no beginner at the game. But that didn't mean that he couldn't be had.

Virgil got behind the wheel and started off. He clicked on the radio, but Willie was quick to note that he didn't call in that he had a suspect in custody. The deal looked better and better.

Tibbs turned north toward the mountains and the unpopulated areas close to the city. Willie knew at once that they weren't headed toward the police station, a fact that both encouraged him and put him doubly on his guard. For almost fifteen minutes the unmarked police vehicle wove its way out of the city.

"What you tryin' to pull off?" Willie asked. His hands were cuffed behind him, but he was lithe enough to get them out in front if he had a chance. Then, cuffed or not, he would be able to give a helluva showing if he had to.

When they reached a deserted area on high ground, Tibbs turned onto a fire ramp and parked his car out of sight. Then he picked up the microphone and reported himself code five without giving his location. That told the dispatcher that he was on stakeout and didn't want to give away his position over the air.

"Ten four," he was reassured, and the radio contact ended.

Tibbs removed the key from the ignition and then turned in his seat to face his prisoner. "What's your name?" he asked.

"The hell with you," Willie answered. He wasn't going to give in that easily.

Virgil pulled out his gun and pointed it straight at Willie's groin.

Willie hesitated for two seconds, no more. His prints were on file and he could easily be IDed. "Willie," he said.

"All right, Willie, I'll tell you just how it is. I know you and who you are. You've been inside, haven't you?"

There was no point in denying it. "Yeah."

"What for?"

"Armed robbery."

"Now, Willie, I'm a cop and I know that you're good for the two eleven tonight at the supermarket—the one where the girl cashier was shot. If I take you in on that, I'm going to look very good."

"You can't prove no damn thing at all," Willie interrupted.

Tibbs remained completely calm. "It doesn't mean a damn thing what I can prove," he said, "because I've got other plans for you. Now I'm going to tell you something. A couple of bums like you came into my town and pulled a job at a small late-night grocery. But they made a mistake. They beat up a friend of mine who was working there. He was white, but I've got white friends too. The judge let him off. They found him a few days later, hanging by his neck in a shed that we only use once a year."

Willie shifted in his seat, listening and trying to think.

"You know, Willie, when they hang them in prison, legally, they put the noose around their necks and then drop them six feet or so, depending on their age and build. They fall through a trap, the sudden stop snaps their necks, and they're dead instantly. They never feel a thing. But this guy didn't die that way. I let him down easily so he would die by strangulation, which is a very tough way to go. And you know what else I did? When he passed out, after all his struggles, I hauled him up, revived him, and when he thought it was all over I did it to him again. And I told him there wouldn't be a second reprieve. So he died twice."

"What kind of a cop you be?" Willie asked. For the first time a tinge of fear colored his voice.

"Just sit there and don't move. If you do, you get 'em blown off," Tibbs continued in the same quiet voice. "What you don't know is that every time a nigger buck like you gets busted, it makes the rest of us look bad. Very bad. All the good black people who've got enough problems without the likes of you. Then there were four guys who picked up a white girl and raped her. It's a funny thing, but it was right in this spot where we are now. The same place, exactly. They got off, too, because the little lady couldn't identify them positively. Well, one of those assholes let on to a friend of mine what he had done."

"You aren't talkin' about the one who got his throat slit, are you?" The prisoner wanted information, urgently. Something new was shaping up in his mind.

"You catch on real fast, Willie. That's good. Tonight you and your buddies ripped off a store. But do you know what else you did? *You grabbed my woman, that's what!*"

For the first time Willie was truly frightened. He was faced with a madman—a madman who was a cop, who had a gun, and who had just admitted committing two grue-some murders. At that moment he believed that Tibbs would actually shoot his groin off and a horrifying fear of mutilation swept everything else out of his mind.

He had to fight back, to say or do something that would stave off this lunatic who had already emasculated one man before cutting his throat. He was faced with the kind of killer who had been called Zodiac in San Francisco, or the Boston Strangler, or . . .

A thought leapt into his mind. He saw a possible card he could play and he used it at once. "Your woman, what if I can get her back for you?" When Tibbs frowned, he added, "Right now."

"Keep talking," Virgil said.

"I can get her back; she ain't been harmed." As he pro-nounced those words he knew that he might have to shop his partner, Ty, but he didn't care. He would make any sacrifice that was necessary. He still hoped that in some way he would manage to get the drop on his captor. If he

157

did, then his revenge would be terrible, but he couldn't bank on that chance.

"You start the car," he said. "I'll tell you where to go."

Tibbs did as he was directed. "They'll be looking for me," Tibbs said. "I'll get them off our tail." Before Willie could respond to that, he picked up the microphone. "This is Tibbs," he said in the clear. "I am ten fifteen, request ten twenty-two, excluding ARGUS."

"To Tibbs, ten four, code seventy-seven."

"Hey, what all that shit, man?" Willie asked. He would have tried to leap from the car if he had not been handcuffed.

"Ease off, brother," Virgil answered him. "I told them I was talking with an informant and that I didn't want any interruption no matter what."

"But why you say all those numbers?"

"So that the guys listening in with sets like the one in your car won't take you for an informant. You're going to take me to my woman, aren't you?"

"Yeah, sure," Willie responded.

Tibbs waved his gun under his nose. "You know what?" he said. "I got a silencer for this thing. You try to fake me out, brother, and you'll spend the rest of your life lookin' at what ain't there. If there *is* any of the rest of your life."

That quieted Willie down. The car rolled on, down toward the central east side of the city. As it did so, Tibbs's transmission was run past the watch commander, who put Sergeant Chris Hagerty on it immediately. "Virgil has a suspect in custody," Lieutenant Perkins told Hagerty, "but he's asked us not to take any further action. Don't ask me why, but he had a reason. He said, 'excluding ARGUS.' Do you know that one?"

"Yes, that's the sheriff's designation for the patrol helicopters. Obviously he didn't want to use that word."

"Thanks. Get our bird on him right away. The dispatcher warned him to watch out for an ambush."

Hagerty was already using the phone. "He could have saved his breath. Virg knows what he's doing." He got his connection. "This is Hagerty. I want the bird up to pick up one of our unmarked units. I'll give you the ten twenty as soon as I have it." That would put the reserve Pasadena chopper in the air within the next minute, ready for action.

Hagerty went to the radio console in the watch sergeant's office and put out a call. "Twenty-four X ray seventeen, give us your ten twenty." Every officer listening would know that there was no such unit on patrol, but somebody who would understand was being asked for his location.

Willie heard the message and asked, "That us, man?"

Tibbs shook his head. "No, but I'll give them some bull anyway." He picked up the microphone. "Ten twenty PCC, plus one."

"What all that mean?"

"I told them I was taking time out to go to the can."

"You sure?"

Tibbs sneered at him. "Look around you, man. You see anybody chasing us?"

Willie did look and saw nothing. Then he spied a marked patrol car coming; it went on past, taking no notice.

At headquarters Hagerty was running to the car lot; he knew that Tibbs would be close to Pasadena City College a minute after his broadcast, and that wasn't too far away up Colorado Boulevard.

On frequency two the helicopter reported that it had the message. The tan car would be hard to pick up at night, but Tibbs would find some way to make it conspicuous. A small fleet of units stood by, alerted and ready to move when directed. They all understood they were to keep out of the way until then.

When Tibbs passed the campus of City College he saw a car coming the other way with its brights on; angrily he flashed his own up and down several times in protest. The helicopter pilot saw it clearly and reported that he had made contact. From that moment on, whatever Tibbs's car did, he would follow it.

"Now listen, and listen good," Willie said. "You and I is gonna make a deal. I get you your woman back and you let me and my buddy go. If you don' do that, man, I'll tell all I know."

Virgil stopped the car and stared at his prisoner with an intensity that was terrifying to see. The policeman was instantly gone and a vicious animal was in his place. "You shut your big mouth," he said. "I won't tell you that again. You say one word about me and I'll kill you and claim self-defense. I'm a cop and nobody will doubt it. And you'll be cold hard dead. You got it?"

"I got it," Willie acknowledged.

"Now if you know what's good for you, you'll take me to my woman—fast!"

Willie struggled with his handcuffs to make himself more comfortable, but there was no way. He knew that when he gave up the hostages, he might die on the spot, but Ty was there and maybe Ty would catch on fast enough. The damned gun was again pointed straight at his groin and he had to save himself first.

When Tibbs stopped before the door of a maintenance shop, the helicopter reported the fact immediately. On frequency two Hagerty ordered the backup to close in yet stay just out of sight.

"Blow your horn real quick three times," Willie said.

Tibbs did as directed, touching the horn just enough to be barely heard each time. The garage door began to open. When it was high enough Virgil drove inside, holding his gun hard against his prisoner's genitals.

He cut to his parking lights immediately, picked up his microphone, held it low and out of sight, and said, "nine ninety-seven." Then, gun in hand, he got out of the car.

He saw the other black man, saw that he, too, was armed and ready for instant action. "Peace, brother," Tibbs said. "I'm your ticket out of here."

That caused Ty to hesitate and drop his gun hand a few inches while he listened.

"I got your partner here," Virgil continued. "You got my woman. I got a car you can use. Now let's talk business."

Ty didn't know who the black stranger was, but he could see Willie in the front seat with him. And Ty was desperate. He lowered his gun.

"*Freeze!*" Tibbs barked.

Ty saw the business end of a gun aimed between his eyes. He was experienced; he knew that his own weapon was useless at that moment. Long before he could raise it and fire, he would be a dead man. He froze.

"Drop it."

Ty had no choice; he let his weapon fall to the floor and raised his arms.

As he did so, the alley was suddenly full of cars. Policemen, lead by Hagerty, poured into the garage. Ty was seized, searched, and cuffed; Willie was dragged out of Tibbs's car and thrown none too gently into a cage-back patrol unit.

As daylight flooded the grimy place, Virgil spun around, looking frantically. He heard a single sound and sprinted for the corner of the room. The first hand he seized belonged to the cashier, who had been crudely bound and gagged. He handed her over to Hagerty, who was already at his side, and then found the second hostage. With surprising strength he literally scooped Miriam up into his arms, tore the gag from her mouth, and kissed her with a fire that ran through his whole body.

18

Chief Robert McGowan sat behind his desk in a calm and judicious manner. Bill Conners and Jim Reynolds sat in chairs against one wall. One other man was also in the room, occupying the corner where the chief usually received his guests. Diane Stone opened the door and announced that Virgil Tibbs was outside.

"Ask him to come in," McGowan said.

Virgil entered quietly, neatly dressed in a black blazer and a pair of light gray slacks. His shoes were immaculately shined and his tie was in the best of taste. "You wanted to see me, sir," he said to his chief.

McGowan set the mood by his quiet tone of voice. "Yes, Virgil, I think we should have a talk. You've met Mr. Reynolds and Mr. Conners, I believe. They're with the government."

Tibbs nodded. "Yes, I have."

"Also," McGowan went on, "I thought it would be a good idea to invite Judge Angelini to join us. Have you met him?"

"No," Virgil answered, "but I've testified in his court many times. Good afternoon, your honor." The two men shook hands.

"Virgil," the chief continued, "as a result of the actions you were involved in yesterday, we've been getting quite a lot of calls. Judge Angelini has been under fire. A lot of what we have been hearing concerns you. So I suggested that we get together and find out what you can tell us."

162

Tibbs felt a sense of relief. He had been prepared for anything from a reprimand to a request for his resignation. He was acutely aware just how far out of line he had been, but at least he was being given a hearing.

"By the way," McGowan added, "after consultation we decided that it was advisable to take Judge Angelini into our confidence concerning the Motamboru family. So you may speak freely. I think we've got the whole story of the holdup, the shooting of the cashier, and the taking of the hostages; you don't need to go into that. What we're specifically interested in are your actions after the two eleven went down."

"All right, sir. I knew that Bob Nakamura was looking after the Motamboru children, so I picked up a plain unit to help in the search for the suspects. Since the rest of the guys in the field didn't know who the second hostage was, or her importance, I made it my number-one priority to get her back safely."

In a minute or two he had covered exactly what he had done; he didn't try to excuse himself for any part of it.

"When you took custody of the suspect in the alley, did you threaten him with physical violence?" the judge asked.

"Definitely, your honor, and, I hope, with conviction. I tried to scare the living hell out of him, and I think that I did."

"Why?"

"Because that type of man doesn't yield to friendly persuasion. Every minute that was passing was increasing the risk to the hostages."

"And it worked," the judge replied.

"Yes, sir, it did. He showed me where the hostages were being held. I managed to put out an 'officer needs help' call when we got there. The rest you know."

There was silence for a moment or two. Then the chief spoke again. "Someone mentioned that you seemed glad to see Mrs. Motamboru when you found her safe and sound."

For a mere moment Virgil's composure cracked a little; then he regained control of himself. "That's right, sir. At the time I forgot that I was a police officer, and allowed myself to just be a man."

"I take it that she didn't resist," McGowan said.

"Not that I noticed, sir."

Another silence settled over them until the judge broke it. "We've been getting complaints from all the usual parties that you violated your prisoner's civil and constitutional rights."

"That accusation, in this instance, is quite true, your honor. I didn't read him Miranda, for one thing, and I did threaten him with physical violence. Will you permit me to offer a suggestion?"

"Go ahead."

"Since he did take me to the place where the hostages were being held, and since his arrest was irregular, perhaps you would consider dropping the kidnapping charge against him. I know that's a federal offense, but perhaps it can be arranged. I'm sure that the D.A. will file on the armed robbery, and that will be enough to hold him. If he is found guilty, it should be good for a long term in the joint."

"I don't quite follow your reasoning," Judge Angelini said. "You feel that we owe this man clemency because of the way you handled him?"

"No, sir. Clemency is entirely up to the courts, and he only cooperated because I had him scared stiff. If possible, I would like to see him released on bail. If there is a legal and proper way to put him back on the street, under close cover without his knowledge, it may help us to resolve the two unsolved homicides we now have."

"You want to use him for bait," McGowan said.

"Yes, sir. I don't think there's too much risk involved. I don't have enough evidence to convict as yet, but I believe I may know who to watch—in other words, who did those killings."

As Virgil Tibbs drove toward his temporary home, his thoughts were confused. He had not particularly enjoyed the session in the chief's office despite the fact that it had worked out better for him than he had allowed himself to hope. McGowan had not said so, but it had been apparent that he had seen the priorities exactly as Virgil had: Getting Miriam Motamboru back safe and sound had overridden every other consideration. He had accomplished that and he didn't for a moment regret the methods he had used; he knew that he had had no other real choice.

He also was infused with the thought that he was no longer the bachelor he had been for so long. He had certainly had female friends, and one of them had moved in with him for a little while, but both of them had realized before very long that it was no go. They were still friends— no more, no less. He had never for a moment felt like a married man, not then. But as he drove eastward on Colorado Boulevard, he could not escape the involuntary sensation that he was going home to what was, at least by proxy, his family.

Miriam met him at the door, as she almost always did, and held out her arm to take his jacket. He slipped it off and gave it to her with a smile of gratitude. Then he carefully put his gun on the shelf above the fireplace, where the children could not reach it but where it could very quickly be retrieved if the need arose.

Miriam kissed him just as though he were the husband he was pretending to be. The shock of her loss was still with her, but the experience she had so recently been through blanketed it to a considerable degree. To Tibbs it was something of a wonder that she kept her poise as well as she did. A lesser woman might have become hysterical, with valid reason, or sunk into a mental depression that would require professional help.

The children burst into the room. Pierre said, "Good evening, sir," with real affection in his voice. Clearly, he had been told all that had happened and his approval of Tibbs came close to hero worship.

Annette hugged him around the knees and looked up in gratitude with her large liquid eyes. She could communicate that way without having to struggle with a language she barely understood.

Virgil tried to take it all in calmly—and failed. He had grown very attached to the family it was still his duty to guard and protect. For a second an odd emotion hit him: If he were going to have children, he would want them to be like these.

By that alchemy that can sometimes pass between a man and a woman, Miriam understood. She looked at Tibbs and said, "They're very proud of you. Please let them admire you; they need it very much."

Virgil sat down on the huge, comfortable davenport and played with the children long enough to make them both happy. Then he went into the downstairs guest bathroom to wash and prepare himself for dinner.

During the soup course Pierre announced that he was going to become a policeman. Tibbs took him very seriously and lectured him on the importance of the lessons he was receiving in lieu of school, and on the almost equal importance of developing his physical abilities. He wondered if it would be possible to take Pierre down and enroll him at the Pasadena judo dojo—he was at an ideal age to start that important training. Regretfully he decided that he could not because too many people would hear his accent and ask him questions he could not answer. Moreover, the family might be leaving for home or some other destination at any time. The death of President Motamboru was bound to change things; he reminded himself again that his assignment could be terminated at any time.

It would be lonesome back in his apartment—presuming that he could move into it again. He correctly assumed that the department would have taken care of that, but it still wouldn't be quite the same. Perhaps he would find the right girl soon, but she would have a very tough handicap in trying to erase the image of Miriam.

"You wouldn't believe what I had to pay at the market for food today," Miriam said. "The prices are going out of sight."

Virgil looked up quickly. "Were you escorted?" he asked.

Miriam nodded. "I made a phone call and someone was there. I don't know who. I didn't see him."

She had prepared chateaubriand with béarnaise sauce that was so good that he was tempted, as he so often was, to overeat. He held himself in check with a real effort and had a very small helping of the dessert. He was grateful when Miriam took the children off to bed so that he had a little time to himself to collect and organize his thoughts.

It was almost an hour later when she rejoined him. She had changed into pajamas and a matching stark white robe. The intimate outfit set off the glow of her dark skin and made her almost indecently attractive. She had good reason to be grateful to him and he knew, without allowing the thought to enter his mind, that if he were to make some sort of an advance to her she would probably feel that she could not refuse.

She brought fresh-brewed coffee from the kitchen and a small plate of imported cookies. When she had prepared Virgil's coffee the way he liked it, she sat down beside him, only inches away.

"I want to talk to you," she said quietly. "Now is a good time because the children are already asleep and they won't stir before morning. They're very good about that."

"I'm quite aware," Tibbs answered. He tried his coffee and, as he had expected, it was superb. "When I get married, will you teach my wife to cook?" he asked suddenly. He didn't think about it; it just came out.

"Yes, if I can."

He knew instinctively that he had said the wrong thing, but the best way to overcome the blunder was to let it pass without comment. He drank a little more coffee and then focused his attention on Miriam, inviting her to go on.

She folded her hands carefully in her lap and looked at them for a moment. Then she faced him with a poise that won his renewed admiration.

"I do not have to tell you," she continued as calmly as before, "that while my husband was alive I would not allow myself to think for a moment about another man. I made a lifetime commitment and I was completely prepared to keep it."

Tibbs said nothing and continued to listen.

"I've only had the news for a few days . . ." At that moment he thought she was going to break. But somehow she hung on and only a single tear on her left cheek betrayed her emotion.

"Only a few days," she repeated, "but I have been preparing myself for it for some time and, as best I could, I prepared the children. You have not lived as I have in Africa. In time we could work out our own problems, but there are outside powers that won't allow us to do so. There are, for example, Cuban troops. Cubans have no business in Africa unless they choose to come as tourists or visitors. But not as a military force. My husband was a man of great courage; he would not desert his people or his country. When I said good-bye to him, I knew then that I would probably never see him again."

She reached over and refilled Tibbs's cup. Then she added a bit more to her own cup to warm up the remaining coffee.

"So you will understand that I have been living with widowhood ever since I left my homeland. I adjusted to it and then prayed every night that it would not become a reality. But it did."

She stopped and drank some coffee. When she set the cup down, she was ready to go on.

"I have been under a very great strain," she said, quite factually, "at times almost more than I could bear. I did my best for the sake of the children, but this last episode almost undid me. Now I feel very strongly the need for some support."

When he drew breath to speak, she held up a hand to stop him. "I am very realistic about some things. I know that I am a woman and that just as an accident of birth made me black it also made me attractive to men. I have been aware for some time that I have found favor with you—if that expression is still used—and I have admired the restraint that you have never failed to observe. There are very few men who would not have tried to, how shall I say, establish a warmer relationship. I have been acutely conscious of what this has cost you and I'm sorry to have

168

laid this additional burden on you."

She stopped once more, but Tibbs sat perfectly still and did not even wish to speak.

She looked at him very steadily. "I know, too, that you understand completely what I am saying. I need your help, your strength, and the comfort that you can give me. There is no other man on earth to whom I would, or could, say this, but I would be very grateful if you would sleep with me tonight."

They drank their coffee together in silence. When they had finished, Miriam took the tray back to the kitchen and, as she always did, washed and put everything away so that the room was left in perfect order.

As Virgil took her upstairs, his arm around her waist and hers around his, he was grateful to God for the healing outlet that had been given to them both.

He undressed slowly in his own room, wondering how long he should wait before going in to her. Instead she came to him, shutting the door quietly behind her. The lights were already off. By the light that filtered in through the windows, he saw her lay her robe aside. When she climbed into bed beside him, it was as if she belonged there.

19

Willie Snodgrass sat in court with the knowledge that he was at that moment a pawn not in control of his own destiny. Once again he'd been busted and now he was in court. He refused to let his mind go further than that. He would not think ahead to prison and the horror that awaited him there.

George and his brother had the first hearing; he did not pay too much attention as questions were asked and answered because he had lost all confidence in George; he, too, had been caught. George was white but that didn't help him deal with Judge Angelini. They were bound over for trial. There was also a federal hold on them for the kidnapping charge, so there was no way they were going to be sprung on bail.

They took Ty next. As Willie watched, the wheels of justice all but rolled over him. He was identified by both of the checkers from the supermarket; one was still in a wheelchair because he had shot her. Ty had been wearing a ski mask, but she claimed that while she had been lying on the floor, she had studied him and had seen that the little finger of his left hand was missing. A cop had shot it off years before; Ty had made him pay with his life for doing it to a black man.

He had been captured while he was holding hostages and he had drawn down on the black cop. That added up to kidnapping and assaulting a peace officer. Lastly, there were two warrants out on him, one from Florida and the other from Michigan. The judge bound him over with a minimum of delay. Then it was Willie's turn.

It was at this point that he began to realize what was about to happen to him. In desperation he eyed every corner of the courtroom, looking for a possible chance to make a breakout. He was naked without a gun or a knife—a proud black man reduced to the status of an animal. He felt no guilt or remorse whatever: Those emotions were unknown to him. He only knew that he was in trouble, deep trouble, and he had to get out of it. As soon as he did, he was going to take care of that black cop.

As Willie watched with concentrated spite, Tibbs was sworn in and took the stand. He was obviously an experienced witness and Willie knew what he was about to say. For a brief moment the vision of a maximum-security prison leaped into his mind and an icy chill of pure terror ran through him. He knew that he was going to end up there, but he couldn't bear to torture himself with the image; if he did, he would go out of his mind. He comforted himself with the thought that it would be a short term. When he got out on parole, he would never trust another white partner; George had let him down, and it was little comfort to know that George was going to prison too. As soon as he got out, Willie thought, he would pull some stickups to bankroll himself and this time he would leave no living witnesses. Corpses couldn't testify.

Automatically Willie assumed his mask of contrite submission, feigning a realization that he had done wrong to society. He could do it so well that he had once fooled a local judge into letting him go free, so he kept hoping that it would work again. He knew he would be bound over, but he would plant the seed that he was a fine young man who had been led astray by bad companions. At the very least it might mean a lighter sentence.

As the hearing began, Willie could not believe his ears. The black cop was a brother after all! He was saying good things about him, for example, about how he had told where the hostages were being held and had shown the way there so they could be released. The judge leaned forward and seemed to be listening sympathetically. Willie responded by hanging his head a little less and trying to look like a reformed man who had seen the light of Jesus. He almost believed it himself when he heard Tibbs describe him as cooperative and apparently anxious to redeem himself.

Then he got it—the black cop was buying his own hide because he knew that if he didn't get Willie off, his own days would be numbered. It didn't matter. It was beginning to look good and Willie would have let them cut off his leg to keep him from going back to prison; there was a convict inside waiting for him who had promised to gouge both his eyes out.

The public defender did not put Willie on the stand. Instead, he made a speech about how Willie had been trapped into becoming part of the salt-and-pepper gang and that he had shown by his actions that he was deserving of the court's mercy.

The idiot judge bought it; he shuffled through some papers and then said he was going to ask for some further reports. He had already heard Willie's probation officer testify that his ward had been working hard in a junkyard and had been doing well up to the moment when his employer had led him back into crime. The alternative would have been the loss of his job, and in his position they were few and far between.

Then a miracle occurred and Willie was released on bail pending a further hearing. There was a small huddle before the bench and then the judge released him, without bail, into the custody of his parole officer. Willie performed the appropriate dramatic gestures, overdoing it a little, but soft judges were a sop for it. After that a few more things were cleared away before Willie Snodgrass walked out a free man.

He had plenty of money. George had insisted that each member of the gang carry a good stash so he would have resources in case they ever had to scatter; in some ways George hadn't been so dumb. But he was still going to prison and Willie clearly wasn't. Freedom felt so good that he chose to walk. He had no idea whatever how expertly he was being shadowed.

In the quiet of the morning, Virgil Tibbs sat in the kitchen and enjoyed a leisurely breakfast. It was his day off and he was determined to make the most of it. Miriam had prepared an omelet for him that was so good he had never tasted anything like it. While she was closeted with the children, giving them their daily lessons, he took the time to read the paper thoroughly.

It was filled with a grim and depressing account of the world's affairs, with few cheerful stories to break the gloom. There were reports of accidents and various disasters: A boat had sunk off Hong Kong; a train had been derailed in Italy as a result of sabotage. An assortment of major crimes also made the news. Armed robbery led the list, but there were many killings and several rapes. It was a composite picture of violence. Many people were opposed to it, but it surrounded them and there was no hiding place. Too often it was spawned by greed, religious differences, and politics; and these causes often tended to overlap. There was nothing whatever about Bakara.

When he had finished reading, he put the paper down and thought while he drank a second cup of coffee. He had heard of the Roaring Twenties and the Depressed Thirties. Would people someday refer to his own era as the Violent Seventies? It went on and on. Bombs blew the limbs off little children in the insane Irish conflict, destroying innocent lives and wiping out the last shred of sympathy for the terrorists' cause. Murder had become almost commonplace and the longest term in any California prison was, in effect, seven years.

Violence had also penetrated his own private life. The family he was nurturing was its victim—first in its own country and now in Pasadena. Miriam was still shaken by her experience. Shaken was hardly the word; it was a wonder that she had kept her sanity.

Once again he was grateful that he was a policeman, able to do at least a small part to preserve a decent society.

That thought did not dilute his appreciation of the day when he could for the moment set aside his responsibilities—despite the fact that his gun was at that moment fitted snugly against his hip.

He interrupted the school session to ask if his temporary family would like to go to Knott's Berry Farm. The enthusiastic response by Pierre and Annette effectively ended the teaching session, but Miriam did not mind. Virgil phoned the special number he had been given and reported his intentions. He was given permission and was told that he would be covered from the moment he arrived at the amusement park. He was instructed exactly where to park his car and at what time.

When he went outside to start the car, he looked up into the sky of an almost perfect day. A line of poetry he had learned in high school came back to him: "God's in his heaven—/All's right with the world." He wanted desperately to believe it, even if for just a little while.

As he drove away from the house, Miriam beside him and the children in back, he fantasized that they were really his family and that their little outing was a usual event. He looked at Miriam and their eyes met. She smiled at him, a soft, gentle smile filled with confidence and warmth. It was a little bit of a shock to him to discover that she was thinking the same thoughts as himself.

Bob Nakamura sat quietly while Dr. William Pierce Smedley expounded on the new campaign he was just launching. The Nisei detective had a gift for presenting a pleasant face that revealed nothing, but inwardly he was agreeing with much that the doctor had to say.

"When people go to vote they see a lot of judges' names," Smedley explained, "but they don't know a damn thing about most of them. So we're going to tell them."

He displayed a large poster on heavy cardboard. At the top it read: THIS JUDGE. Immediately below the headline there was a portrait of a jurist on the bench. Just below that there was another line of bold type: FREED THESE

174

MEN. The rest of the space was filled with mug shots of convicted criminals.

"When we put these up all over the county," Smedley continued, "watch and see what happens. When the public learned about Nixon at last, you know what happened to him. He became the most disgraced man in history."

"What about the good judges?" Bob asked.

Smedley produced another poster similar in design to the first. But the second headline read: SENT THESE MEN TO PRISON.

"It isn't a question of like or dislike," the doctor explained. "It's a question of competence and responsibility. Actually, I know and personally like one of the judges to whom we're going to give the treatment. But he's far too soft on crime, so he'll have to pay the price."

"How about our chief justice?" Bob's face was a study in innocence.

"Don't worry," Smedley snapped. "We're going to get to her shortly."

"What do you think about the two criminals who were murdered here? Those cases are still unsolved, you know."

Smedley slapped his palms against the top of his desk. "I can't help you, but even if I could I'm not sure I would. I would never institute that sort of thing, but the law provides for justifiable homicide and in my opinion those two killings come pretty close to the mark."

Rubin Goldfarb impressed Bob Nakamura as the sort of man whiskey manufacturers like to feature in their ads. He was rugged-looking, definitely virile, and quite clearly an active type. Since most of his properties were well managed for him, he had plenty of leisure time. He was extroverted enough to be willing to talk on almost any subject. He received the Nisei detective without an appointment and with every sign of affability. As he settled himself in his luxurious office chair, he epitomized a kind of success that he knew most men would envy.

From an elaborate bar he had his secretary prepare two

of his own personal tropical concoctions. Drinking on duty was strictly banned, but Bob did not hesitate to make an exception. It helped to suggest that the call was largely a routine one—and that was just what he wanted. Also, it would have been conspicuously rude to have declined the fancy cocktail that was put in his hand. There were some men, Bob knew, who were highly offended if someone refused to join them in a drink.

In this pleasant atmosphere the two men talked easily, so that Goldfarb had no idea how skillfully he was being questioned. When the subject of education came up, Goldfarb revealed the fact that he had been elected to Phi Beta Kappa, although he didn't wear the key. He had majored in English, something that Bob noted with special interest. He had also played on the football team and could still run a most respectable mile. He was quite a guy.

When Bob at last left, he had acquired a considerable amount of information, some of which might be of future use. He was interested in the fact that Willis Raymond, the clerk who had been pistol-whipped, had been promoted again and given a substantial raise.

Since there was still time in his working day, Bob drove a few blocks to the coffee shop where Raymond would be holding forth. When he arrived, he sat down in a booth, ordered coffee, and asked to see the manager.

When Raymond appeared, Bob observed that he'd had some good restorative dentistry. It was obvious to Bob that in his new job Raymond was carefully cultivating a pleasing manner. He walked up to the table very professionally and asked what he could do for him.

Bob put on one of his most agreeable faces and produced his badge. "I wonder if you could take a minute to join me in a cup of coffee?" he asked, making it sound like an invitation.

In response, Raymond sat down and faced the policeman with every evidence of poise and confidence. Within a minute or two he was talking easily, perhaps a bit pleased that he had been looked up for his opinion. Bob handled him carefully, building a rapport and keeping him at ease.

Then, quite casually, he turned to the topic of Raymond's rapid rise in the Goldfarb organization. His salary was more than twice what he had earned when he had been night manager of the small grocery where he had been injured.

By some deft twists in the conversation, Bob brought it down to a confidential, man-to-man basis. "Look," he said, "sometimes we like to know what's going on just so we can protect certain citizens—people who are important in the community. Then, if some old biddy files a complaint with us, we'll know just how to handle it. We don't like to bother good people if it can be helped."

"I understand," Raymond said.

"I'm glad you do," Bob continued. "Now let me level with you. We've noticed that you've come a long way with Mr. Goldfarb since the incident when those blacks smashed you up. Part of it is undoubtedly due to your ability, part of it may be that he's making it up to you for what you've gone through, but I have a hunch that there's a little more to it. Am I right?"

Raymond looked at him for a moment before answering. "You aren't trying to bust my boss, are you?" he asked.

"What could we bust him for?" Bob asked in return.

"Well, you know, he gets on pretty well with women."

"I should think so," Bob said. "I wish I had his looks. As far as we're concerned, as long as the women he chooses are adults and he's discreet about it, we couldn't care less."

Raymond looked around him to be sure that they weren't being overheard. "Well, he's quite a ladies' man and he likes variety; he told me that himself."

"He likes to cut notches in the bedpost," Bob said.

"He sure does." Raymond leaned closer. "You want to know something? He's had more than four hundred women. Four hundred! But he's got the looks, he's got the dough, and that's what does it."

"Sort of his hobby."

"Exactly. Well, that's where I've been coming in. A lot of good-looking babes come in here. When I spot one that looks like she might swing a little, I kind of play up to her and if she responds I tell her she should see my boss, that he's an ex-footballer, a wealthy guy, and that he likes to buy things for nice girls. I get a nice bonus from him—in cash, you understand."

"Sure," Bob said.

"So that's why he's been taking good care of me. And I can't complain. I have my share of the fun, too, sometimes."

That answered a lot of questions. As Bob drove back to his office, he turned the whole interview over in his mind. When he was back on the second floor of the old police building, he wrote up his findings in an abbreviated, lucid style and left the results on Virgil's desk.

Willie Snodgrass decided to stay in Pasadena for a little while. Despite the fact that he was required to remain within the jurisdiction of the court, he had given some thought to going back to the junkyard and searching for the stashed money that was rightfully his. George was out of the way and would be for some time. Willie was not much of a thinker, but he did realize that the junkyard was a large and complicated place where there had to be literally thousands of hiding places where money could be stashed; it would probably take him a very long time to find it. Also, in view of the fact that George had been busted, he realized that the police would have been over the junkyard with teams of men and whatever there was to be found would now be in their possession.

It was a small fortune lost, but more could be gotten when the time came. For the moment he had all the money he needed, and he was not one to plan very far ahead. Also, the cops were leaving him alone—or so he thought. He was enjoying himself. When he had to, he would get a gun and go back to work, but there was no rush about that. He might even be able to get some of the money from the junkyard by claiming that it was back wages due him. He had not for one moment forgotten the black cop, but the fact that he was out on the street and not in jail was due to the same man, so he was playing it cool. After all the charges against him had been dismissed he could look into that matter. For the time being he was content to be a good boy and enjoy the girl it had been his good fortune to find. He completely forgot about the brutal murders of two other criminals that had taken place so recently.

20

Covering Willie Snodgrass almost night and day was one of the most exacting and dangerous jobs that Virgil Tibbs had ever drawn. It had been his idea and he had known at the time that he would draw the assignment, but that didn't make his task easier. He didn't even carry a walkie-talkie with him so that he could summon backup help if needed; for that he had to rely on the public telephone system. He therefore went about his work with a number of dimes in his pocket and a continuing prayer in his heart.

He knew the dangers of the business he had chosen; they had never concerned him too much because he knew that he could take care of himself and that he was a member of a highly efficient team—but that had been before he had met Miriam Motamboru. No decision had as yet been made as to what was to be done with her, but he knew that his role as her husband would soon have to end. He had no idea what would become of her or her children, so he cherished every day that he could share with them. For the first time his own survival became a matter of genuine concern.

He was working under cover in the black section of Pasadena. He was well known there, but keeping out of sight considerably improved his odds. Some of the people who knew him could be counted on to keep their mouths shut. All of the law-abiding people in the area would never betray him, and that was a majority he could count on. They didn't want a criminal in their midst; they, too, sent their children to school and went alone to the stores to buy food and other commodities.

One of the working girls knew Tibbs well. Technically he could have busted her a number of times for prostitution, but he had not done so because she was a helpful and accurate informant. Murderers, armed robbers, rapists, child molesters, and similar heavy offenders got no sympathy from her. It was not generally known that she had an eight-year-old daughter, the product of a disastrous marriage. She was very much concerned for her child's welfare; the fact that she made herself available on street corners did not concern the police department too much. None of her clients ever complained that they had been rolled; and in other respects she kept her nose clean. When she had enough saved, she was going to put her daughter into a private school and then go to beauty operator's college. She knew most of the cops in her area and she knew that none of them would blow the whistle on her.

She was not the girl who was taking care of Willie Snodgrass—she was not available to the likes of him—but she did know what was going on and what kind of a man he was. She knew who was meeting his physical needs and the risk that girl was running, but she had a very expensive habit to support and the cost of heroin, like everything else, was going through the roof.

Through her Tibbs learned a great deal about the habits of Willie Snodgrass; it helped him in maintaining a close cover without Willie's knowledge. A great deal of time and money was being spent to keep track of every move Snodgrass made.

Virgil wore the kind of old clothes that matched his cover—that of an occasional laborer who did enough work to keep himself in funds, but not much more. He hung around the cheap restaurants and fast-food stands where Willie stopped in frequently. If Willie were to recognize him, there could be heavy trouble at once, but Tibbs's caution and experience paid off; he trailed Willie almost like his own shadow and not once did his subject suspect that he was there. Bob Nakamura was helping to keep a close watch on certain other people so that, if possible, Tibbs could be forewarned.

The first break came when a regular white patrol unit rolled code three down a street that had been agreed upon. Everyone within three or four blocks could hear the electronic siren, and although the unit was not going too fast, not one civilian expected that it was anything more than a routine police action. When Virgil heard it, he disappeared between two buildings and then ran, out of sight, as fast as he could to the old Ford he had parked on a side street. It was a cover car borrowed from a used-car lot and changed every few days.

Tibbs unlocked it, jumped inside, and unlocked the glove compartment. He took out the police walkie-talkie, turned to channel two, and reported in.

He was quickly told that certain movements had been observed. The words made his heart pound faster; he had been waiting patiently several days for this, very long days in which he had hardly had any sleep at all. He uttered a silent prayer that it was not a false alarm and then started up the car. He drove to where he could observe Willie's lodging, risking the added exposure since there was no other way. He was not taking too much of a chance; the car fitted his disguise and it fitted the neighborhood.

With his hand radio he gave his code five position and the license plate number of the car he was in. In a matter of seconds several patrol units in his vicinity knew that he was on stakeout and had a description of his vehicle. Two unmarked cars left the station with detective personnel and parked far enough away to avoid arousing suspicion, yet close enough to cover him in a minute flat if that became necessary.

Tibbs gave code six, which advised that he was leaving his vehicle to investigate, and dissolved into the background. He kept his radio out of sight. If he'd remained in his car too long, the sharp eyes of the neighborhood would have made him in short order; that was a risk he did not dare to take.

When he saw a car stop and a white man get out, he

watched intently until he saw the man turn into the doorway of the place where Willie was staying. Then he used his radio once more. "It looks like it's going down," he reported.

A patrol unit went cruising past, as one did every few minutes, and disappeared up the street. Virgil had spotted the driver, Lieutenant Dallas Perkins, and knew that he had heavy support if he needed it. Seated beside Perkins was Mary Goldie, who worked juvenile. Anyone seeing the two of them in the car would have taken her for a ride around; she didn't look the least bit like a cop.

Ben Hetherington gave him a quick call from one of the unmarked units. Virgil responded by giving the license plate number and description of the car that parked close by. The owner's ID came back within seconds, but it was not anyone Virgil recognized.

Five minutes later Bob Nakamura supplied some further information via radio. Tibbs acknowledged it and then maintained quiet. He moved his position just in case anyone had taken notice of him; he concealed his radio under his jacket and wandered down the street in a way that would excite the minimum of suspicion.

A patrol unit came down the street, flashed a spotlight on him, and pulled over. Two officers got out and asked him to produce his ID. It was a common sight in the neighborhood, and getting hassled by the cops was a mark of respectability. Tibbs went through all the motions and permitted himself to be patted down. The officer gave no hint of the radio under Tibbs's jacket or the service gun carefully concealed against his hip. In a low voice he asked, "What do you need?"

"I'm sure it's going down," Tibbs answered. "The car fifty feet ahead of you is the suspect vehicle. I want it followed without the driver knowing. Pass the word."

"Will do, Virg."

He was still apparently being interrogated when Willie Snodgrass came walking down the street. The patrol officer who was talking to Tibbs saw him coming and recognized him from the picture that was posted in the station. Without a moment's hesitation he spun Tibbs around so that he faced the car. Virgil put his hands up on the roof of the car and spread his legs slightly. The patrol officer who was supposedly handling him used his own right foot to kick his legs further back and farther apart; then he began to go through Tibbs's pockets.

The performance continued while Willie, giving it a quick glance, turned into the doorway of his rooming house. Then the search ended and the officer got back into his car, apparently satisfied. As he drove away, Tibbs hurled a remark after him that was exactly right to express indignation without inviting more trouble.

As far as any spectators were concerned, that was proof positive that Tibbs, whoever he was, was unarmed and no threat to anyone. As a matter of fact, the man who had gone into Willie Snodgrass' place and had let himself into his room did see most of it and was suitably pleased when the patrol car drove away. He did not see the man who had been stopped go away and he did not care. The incident was closed. He did see Willie coming and got himself ready. When Willie turned the lights on, he would find him, gun in hand, ready to talk. The gun would insure Willie's cooperation because even if he was carrying one himself, he would not have the time to reach for it and he knew it.

It was being done a little differently this time, even a little better than before. It worked just as he had planned. Willie came in, turned on the light, and froze.

"Hello, Willie," the visitor said. "Don't be frightened. I just want to have a little talk."

"You a cop?" Willie demanded.

The visitor shook his head, grinning as he did so. "I'm no cop," he answered, and his words carried conviction.

"Then what you want with me?"

The invisible bug that had been planted in the room by court permission caught every intonation.

"First of all, Willie, I want to make sure you aren't packing. Turn around and lean against the wall."

Willie assumed the proper position and was felt down

none too gently. The visitor checked his groin area, which many cops hesitated to do. That told Willie that the man he was up against was a pro and he knew he would have to watch his step.

"Have you got a gun stashed someplace?" the visitor asked.

"No, I ain't got no gun."

"That's all right; we've got plenty."

That was the first clue Willie had. He was not bright, but he understood that he was being recruited for something. "You connected?" he asked.

"Nope. We've got our own little organization. Not one of us has ever been busted for anything. You get it?"

Willie understood. Not having a record could be a tremendous asset in any kind of operation. He wanted to ask questions, but he knew that he would be told very shortly what was wanted of him.

"We know all about you," the visitor said. "More than the cops do. You were pretty smart to get yourself out of that kidnapping rap when you knew it had gone sour. We need you for about three days' work."

"When?" Willie asked.

"Very soon, Willie, and it's worth ten grand to you. Can you use that kind of money?"

"That's a dumb question," Willie answered. "What you want, and what's the risk?"

The white man shrugged. "There's a risk—there's always a risk—but, like I told you, none of us has ever been busted. Nobody will see you; if they do, you're just another black man and that's all they'll know."

"They know me around here," Willie said.

The other man waved his gun up and down a little just to emphasize that he was in charge. "It won't be around here. You won't be gone long and nobody's going to even know you ever left the city. We can give a girl a hundred bucks to say that you were with her all night."

That impressed Willie; any outfit that would hand out a big bill just to cover a little thing like that had to be big time. And he had known for years that he was real big time material.

"What kind of job?" he asked.

The white man smiled. "One reason that none of us ever got caught was because we kept our traps shut. And nobody that ever worked for us got made on any job we ever ran. For the same reason."

"I still gotta know what it's all about." Willie was not in the mood to take any chances either.

The white man considered that for a moment. "Well, maybe we'll tell you that; you've got a right to know. There's a boat coming in. Never mind when or where, but it's ours. It's got a very valuable cargo. We're going to need some help in getting it unloaded. When that's done, we have to make a delivery. We never go to the same place twice. We won't get stopped, but if we do you're just the laborer we hired; you haven't any idea what we're carrying."

"It won't go," Willie said. "If they pick me up outside this town, I go back inside for breaking parole. And I got a heavy record. They'll know."

The white man stood up and flashed a sudden smile. "That's absolutely right, Willie, I just wanted to be sure myself that you are a bright buy. Forget that boat part, that's crap. You're O.K. If I approved of you, the boss said he wanted to see you right now, here in Pasadena. There's no risk at all. You make two hundred just to talk to him. That's to make sure you forget about it afterward if it doesn't work out." The speaker reached inside his coat, took out his wallet, and counted out ten twenty-dollar bills. Almost carelessly he folded them and handed them over. "Is that enough to keep you quiet?" he asked.

"I can't afford to talk," Willie answered. He put the money in his pocket and then got to his feet. "Let's go," he said.

When Willie came out into the street, three members of the Pasadena Police Department saw him. As he walked to the parked car, they were on alert. When the white man joined him, they were ready for action.

The inconspicuous car drove away, the white man at the wheel. When he looked carefully in his rear-view mirror, he saw that no one was following him. He did not see, or hear, the helicopter that was four hundred feet overhead. He never dreamed that the roof of his car had been sprayed with an invisible paint that the infrared detector in the helicopter could follow through the blackest night.

When the driver turned his first corner westward, Virgil Tibbs pulled his own nondescript car away from the curb and set off in pursuit. He drove at a moderate speed, his hand radio beside him on the seat. The running report on channel two kept him up to date. He knew when the car turned down toward the Rose Bowl and started northward toward the wilder section of the huge park in the Arroyo Seco. He knew that spot well; the last time he had been there it had been on a Sunday morning and the body of a young woman had just been discovered by a scoutmaster out on a hike with his troop. He was at that moment even more sure that the caper was going down.

He saw his working-girl informant standing on her assigned corner and had an inspiration. He picked her up as though it were purely a matter of business. She hopped in, closed the door behind her, and then asked. "What's up, Virgil?"

"I thought it would look better if I had my girl friend with me."

"I dig," she answered, and lighted a cigarette. "You owe me one."

"Count on it."

"What's it all about?"

"Did you see a car go past?"

"So. It's Willie Snodgrass."

"He may be on the verge of doing an unwise thing. If so, I plan to prevent it."

"I hope you make it. He's been giving Edna too hard a time for what he pays her. He wants it all three ways."

That didn't call for any comment and Virgil offered none.

187

Presently his radio came on again and he listened intently. Then he picked it up. "I'll need some backup," he said. "But let me go in on it alone. Stay close but out of sight."

Mary Goldie's voice cut in. "Watch it, Virg, the Caucasian is packing. I saw it when he came out of the doorway. It's in his belt on the right-hand side."

"Ten four," Tibbs answered. He had expected that he would be facing at least one gun; even if Willie wasn't armed, others might be.

He reported that he had a civilian female in the car with him. That was understood; she would be kept out of things and given protection if necessary.

Close to the north end of the park driveway the suspect car pulled over. The driver got out, raised the hood, and positioned the rod that held it open. It was a simple yet effective device that explained why the car had stopped there and why the driver wasn't with it; presumably he had walked away to get help.

"Let's go," he said to Willie. "Don't worry. We never use the same place twice, and we haven't been followed; I saw to that."

Willie knew that his guide had a gun, but as long as he walked in front it was all right. Willie was quick and powerful; he was a trained street fighter. He felt completely safe and no cops would be anywhere down there.

When the two men had disappeared over a small rill, Virgil Tibbs parked his own car two hundred feet behind the vehicle he had been following. Overhead the helicopter was missing nothing, but soon the suspects would be lost in the thick brush and trees. The observer reported that fact by radio.

Two unmarked units pulled up and dropped off three men. Then the cars drove away before they attracted any attention. One of the plainclothes officers spoke to the girl that Tibbs had left in his vehicle. Normally he worked burglary and he hadn't met her. "We know about you, miss," he told her. "You may not see us, but we'll be close by in case you need us. We won't leave you alone and unprotected at night."

188

"Big deal," she answered.

Virgil had not been expecting this kind of an operation when he had dressed that morning, but he did have on a pair of old track shoes. They were convenient, but they didn't guarantee that he might not step on a twig or kick a stone and betray himself, so as he went up the pathway into the growing darkness he exercised maximum caution. He couldn't risk taking his radio: it might go on at any moment. He checked his weapon, but he left it where it was in order to keep his hands free; if he had to push his way through shrubbery, that would be the better way.

Whatever the situation might be, he did not expect that Willie would be glad to see him—not unless things went a lot further than Tibbs intended to let them go. He could not hear any evidence of backup behind him, but he had to go on the assumption that it was there. Presumably the others were being as cautious as he was.

At the top of the rill he dropped down into a prone position so that he wouldn't be outlined against the sky in case anyone was looking in that direction. Ahead of him he saw a little glimmer of light and heard some sounds that made him tense up despite himself. There could be several people gathered and they would not waste any time. It was his move and it would have to be fast.

He got to his feet and went toward the light swiftly and silently. In forty seconds he could begin to hear what was being said; soon after that he was positioned very close to the scene, where he was just safely out of sight. He measured distances carefully with his eyes and planned his path in case he had to take rapid action. It might not be necessary, but he could not afford to take any chances whatever with the people he was dealing with. The fact that he was a policeman would carry very little weight if they found it necessary to protect their own positions.

He heard a voice that he recognized and knew that he had arrived at precisely the right time. He saw that Willie was standing facing the speaker; all he could see of him was his back. The Caucasian who had brought him to the

189

rendezvous was standing in profile, his gun pointed at Willie. It was steady and fixed; the man who held it knew how to use it.

"Now I want you to understand something," the speaker went on. "If you make one move—any kind at all—my friend here is going to shoot you through the kneecap. Do you know how much that hurts? It'll damn near kill you with pain. That will be to get your attention. You can scream all you want because no one will hear you and we'll be long gone—after you've been shot again in the guts. I've seen men die that have been shot that way and, believe me, it's one of the hardest ways to go."

"You're shitting me," Willie said. "I know you. You're a cop."

The speaker laughed. "No, Willie, I'm not a cop, but just suppose I were. That isn't my service gun; it's a special that can't be traced. We could knock you off and that would be all there was to it."

"You ain't gonna hang me from no tree," Willie asserted. "I'll take my chances with that gun, but I ain't so dumb as you think. Right now you got big trouble."

"I didn't say we were going to hang you, Willie. We're going to put a rope around your neck and ask you some questions. If we like the answers, we'll add three more bills to the two you already have and you can go home five hundred dollars richer for no work at all."

"You wanna ask somethin', you ask. But no rope!"

Two other men who appeared from nowhere came up on Willie from behind and expertly kicked his feet from beneath him. As soon as he was down, they threw a strap around him and pinioned his arms against his sides.

Willie struggled hard, but the two men knew exactly what they were doing. Within a second or two they had the strap pulled tight. Then one of them stood up, jumped, and pulled down a noose that had been concealed just out of sight. It was not a cowboy-type knot, but a running loop made from a rope with an eyelet at the end. As Willie was hoisted to his feet, the man who had been doing the talking moved to his left and took hold of the other end of the rope. The noose was quickly dropped over Willie's head. As soon as it was, the man in charge pulled on his end and tightened it. He pulled so hard that Willie was helpless, his head forced over to one side.

Willie had lived with violence the greater part of his short life and he knew how to play the odds. The noose was not so tight that he could not speak. "What you wanna ask?" he said.

"That's fine, Willie, I knew you'd see it our way. I'm sorry we had to play rough, but you know how it is."

"I know," Willie answered. In his imagination he was already atop his tormentor with a knife in his hand. And what he was going to do to that white bastard almost pumped the fear out of him. He had been up against tougher things in prison. These freaks were going to let him go; in the joint he would have been in for it. The men inside knew what being tough really meant. They had stood him up just once, and that once had been enough.

"Actually, Willie, I don't think we have any questions right now. But I'll explain something to you. You shot a white girl in the food market. The fact that she was white isn't important, but the fact that you shot her in cold blood, just like that, when she hadn't done a thing to you is why you're here right now."

It was hard for Willie to talk, but he managed. "I didn't hit her; my partner did. I'm out because I cooperated."

The voice went implacably on, ignoring what he had said. "You're an example of the miscarriage of justice, Willie. You should be in a nice tight cell for the rest of your natural life, but the soft-hearted judge let you out. And don't try to tell me you've reformed; you came here tonight to take on another job. And you're a kidnapper. I know you showed where the victims were, but that was only to save your own worthless hide."

Willie had had enough of that. "What you want me to do?" he asked. He was convinced that the man talking to him was mad, but he would humor him until he could get out of the mess he was in.

"Nothing at all, Willie. We just want you to understand

what we're doing. The courts didn't deal with you properly, so we will. We're not nice men, Willie, but we do good work. Five minutes from now you'll be dead, executed as you deserve to be. You understand, in five minutes you'll be dead."

"I don't think so," Virgil said. He walked calmly forward. If he had had his gun in his hand he might have been in greater danger, but the fact that his hands were empty worked in his favor. He had created a shock, just as he had intended.

He turned quite calmly to the speaker. "I agree that Willie isn't much of a benefit to society, Mr. Goldfarb, but the days of the vigilantes are over."

"Where the hell did you come from?" It was Willis Raymond who asked him that. For the moment he lowered the gun he had been pointing at Willie Snodgrass. His knees were shaking and his voice was a little unnatural.

"I've been with you all along, Willis." He turned and looked toward the other two men, both of whom he had never seen before. "Some more employees of yours, Mr. Goldfarb?" he asked.

"You might say that. Now what do you propose to do? Are you going to try and convince me that Willie Snodgrass is worth laying down your life to rescue?"

"Let's not be dramatic," Virgil answered. "We've had too much of that as it is."

Willis Raymond was not as cool. He was barely able to control himself, but he had to know something. "How did you find out?" he asked.

"You told me yourself when I came to call on you. I told you that the man who had pistol-whipped you was dead by hanging. You corrected me and said that it was the other man. There was no way you could have known that unless you had actually seen the execution or viewed the body afterward, which you didn't do—I checked. You gave yourself completely away with that one statement."

The situation was tense, too much so for Tibbs to draw even one comfortable breath. He kept his cool because there was no other possible way he could avoid disaster.

Willis Raymond had a gun in his hand ready for use. If it came to a shooting contest, there was no way that Virgil could get his own weapon out in time if the man facing him knew what to do with his own gun. The way he was handling it suggested strongly that he did.

With a calm that matched Tibbs's own, Rubin Goldfarb took command of the situation. "Mr. Tibbs," he said. "You have stumbled onto something here that could be very dangerous to you. I don't know how you found us, but I do know that you are a very intelligent man. In that capacity, I don't believe that you would wish back to life the man whom you helped cut down or the rapist who destroyed the life of poor, helpless Emily Myerson. I dealt with them as they deserved, informally but effectively. And nobody found out who we are or how we do our work."

"I did," Tibbs said. "You slipped up too. Very slightly, but it was enough."

Despite the frozen tableau and the extreme discomfort of Willie Snodgrass, Tibbs played out his part just as he had planned. "Mr. Goldfarb, you are a highly educated man, but on one small point you were too well informed. Hanging. It's an unusual word in the English language. The past tense for inanimate objects is 'hung,' but when it's used as a method of execution, it's 'hanged.' When we talked briefly about it, you said 'hanged' properly. Then I deliberately said that the man had been hung and you corrected me; you called it 'hanged' once more."

"You're quibbling, Mr. Tibbs. We have better things to do."

Virgil shook his head. "It was a very small point, but I had already noted that whoever had done the first execution knew a great deal about hanging as the British developed it. Hence your use of the loop, rather than the awkward strangling noose. Also, you borrowed the memoirs of Albert Pierrepont, the famous hangman, from the library. I checked the records. That wasn't proof, of course, but it did strongly suggest to me that you were involved."

"I think it's time for us to make a deal," Goldfarb said.

"I can't afford exposure, even though practically the whole population of Pasadena is behind me—I know that. What do you propose?"

Tibbs shook his head. "I'm sorry to cut short your career, but you are all under arrest."

Willis Raymond raised his gun and began to aim. From a standing position Tibbs exploded into action. He threw himself forward, his right arm curved over his head. He did an expert Aikido roll that took him forward and made him an almost impossible target at the same time. He came up on his feet a little more than a yard in front of Raymond; with a perfectly delivered front snap kick, he knocked the weapon out of Raymond's hand. The whole thing took less than three seconds, but it abruptly changed the situation. Willis dropped to his knees to recover his gun, but Virgil stood over him, his own weapon drawn. "Let go of that rope," he ordered, "and freeze."

For a few seconds no one moved; it was one man against four, with Willie a doubtful asset either way; even with the rope slackened, his arms were still securely strapped to his sides.

Under those strained circumstances, Rubin Goldfarb showed almost inhuman calm. "Willis," he said, "you should know better than to threaten Mr. Tibbs with a gun. He's a professional and you're an amateur." He turned his head slightly and looked at Tibbs with no fear visible on his face. Then he spoke once more. "You know that we're on the same side. I've taken two human abominations off the streets of this city when the courts failed to back you up. Both were proven murderers. Now, sir, it's time for us, as gentlemen who know how to keep our mouths shut, to make a deal."

At that point the voice of Lieutenant Dallas Perkins was heard loud and clear. He appeared from directly behind Raymond; he also had his service revolver in his hand. "There won't be any deal," he announced. "You might note the helicopter overhead—it's been there for some time. And there are quite a few of us here now; eight to be exact. I strongly advise you to come quietly."

As he spoke, three other officers stepped into sight. "Do we need to discuss this any further?" Perkins asked.

Goldfarb shook his head. "I don't see any point in that at the moment. Don't bother to read us our rights. I know them. I do want to call my lawyer."

"You can do that at the station," Perkins told him. "Let's go."

21

A little past nine-thirty the doorbell rang at the house where Miriam Motamboru was living with her children. She looked first at the image on the small closed-circuit TV screen beside the door before she opened it to greet the smiling face of Bob Nakamura. Beside him was his wife, Amiko, who still looked twenty-five although she was well past that point.

"Come in," Miriam said. "I'm so glad to have some company. I'll have hot coffee in just a minute or two. Sit down and be comfortable."

The Nakamuras came in, but they did not sit down. "We're the baby-sitters," Amiko explained. "We're taking our kids for an outing and we came to collect yours. It's Bob's day off."

"Is it all right?" Miriam asked. A shadow of worry crossed her face as she spoke.

Bob nodded. "Yes, it's all cleared. No problem."

"That's wonderful," Miriam said. "Mine are getting stir crazy—I learned that expression from Virgil." She raised her voice and called her children. She could have saved herself the trouble; they presented themselves at once from the staircase where they had been impatiently listening.

"Your uncle Bob and aunt Amiko are going to take you out for the day," she explained. "They have Bob junior and Harriet with them, so you'll have a wonderful time."

There was no problem at all in getting the children ready; they were all too eager. "I hope I can live up to the

196

uncle bit," Bob commented. "They don't look as Japanese as I do."

"They don't know the difference and they don't care," Miriam answered. "The children never have any trouble at all. It's the adults who foul things up." She stopped and shook her head. "I've got to watch myself; I'm getting more Americanized every day."

She herded her small brood outside and saw Pierre and Annette into the car. Before the vehicle was out of the driveway, Pierre was doing his best to talk English with Bob junior, who was close to his own age. Annette, for the moment, was sitting still next to Harriet Nakamura, but that quiet would not last for long. Miriam went back inside and shut the door.

She was listening to the eleven o'clock news on the radio in the kitchen when she heard Virgil come in the front door; by the time he had his key in the lock, she knew who it was. She hurried out to meet him. He had never come home at that hour before. If anything was wrong, she wanted to be at his side.

Virgil's greeting was warm yet restrained. She took the coat he had worn to court and kissed him. Then she asked the question she could no longer avoid. "Is anything wrong?"

Virgil sat down and smiled at her, restoring her confidence that at least some things were right in the world. "It was all over very fast," he said. "So I came home. I have the rest of the day off. Did Bob pick up the kids?"

"About two hours ago. They were very happy. So we have the place to ourselves. Now tell me all about it."

"You don't have a cup of coffee, do you?"

Miriam hurried to the kitchen and was back quickly with coffee she had made for herself.

Virgil took the cup and sipped the coffee gratefully. "Willie Snodgrass copped out to three counts of armed robbery," he told her. "He hasn't been sentenced, but he's looking at a good ten years at least." He turned to look at the woman who had become a part of his life despite his every effort to prevent it. "I can't feel sorry for him, Miriam. It's true that we put him back on the street for bait and it worked. He had a very nasty time for a few minutes before we sprung him from his captors, but he brought it on himself. He went willingly because he was offered ten thousand dollars for three days' work; we've got a tape of the conversation. He took it immediately, knowing that it had to be a criminal enterprise. If he'd had the sense to turn it down, he would have been in the clear and the court might have been lenient. But Willie couldn't wait to return to the only life he knows, so it's back to the joint for him. Thank God he'll be out of our hair for a few years at least."

"I can't feel sorry for him either," Miriam said.

Virgil did not respond to that; instead, he remained unusually quiet. He drank his coffee and looked about the room as though he had never seen it before. Miriam knew at once that something very serious was on his mind and she prepared herself for whatever might be coming.

"I have some news for you," he said finally. "I want you to take it just as I'm going to give it to you—as calmly as you can."

Miriam folded her hands in her lap. "I'm ready," she said.

"It's in two parts. First of all, there is a rumor, a very faint one, that your husband may still be alive. I wouldn't give it more than 5 per cent, but it rests on the fact that a body that was identified as his didn't check out. That's all there is to it. If he is alive, no one has seen him and, frankly, a man of his prominence couldn't simply disappear in the heart of Africa if he were alive and well—at least I don't think so. But there was that misidentification, and that you're entitled to know."

"Who told you?" Miriam asked.

"Bill Conners of the State Department. We had a phone conversation early this morning and then I saw him briefly before I came home."

"What is the other part?" Miriam asked. She was not impatient; she was only doing her best to make it easy for him.

Tibbs pressed his lips together and made his expression appear as unconcerned as he could. "There's been some high-level horse trading going on that I don't know anything about," he said in an even and controlled voice. "Somehow, some guarantees have been worked out. I don't know any of the details, but they're going to move you to Switzerland. They have a chateau there where you will be perfectly safe. The Swiss are good about remaining neutral, and you've been officially invited."

He'd said it and it was over. Miriam sat very still while she put the news together in her mind. She did not trust herself to say anything. She had no idea how long it was before Virgil spoke to her again because time had lost much of its meaning. She was almost inured to shock, so the fresh waves of both joy and despair washed against her without making any real impression. At that moment Virgil was the key; whatever else he might have to tell her would probably let her know her fate. She was too emotionally exhausted to fight anymore. She was anxious for him to go on, but she was fearful of what his words might be.

"Miriam, they're going to take you and the children to Switzerland in a few days. The story will be put out that you have been staying with friends who were careful to respect your privacy. That's all. Nothing about the Pasadena Police; in fact, that city probably won't be mentioned." He turned and looked at her. "I'm afraid you'll have to go," he added.

She swallowed and nodded. "I know," she responded. "I don't want to."

Virgil laid a hand on her shoulder. "Miriam, I shouldn't tell this to you, but I have been living a dream. I had no right to, but I did. I allowed myself to think of you as my own wife and your children as our children because I love you so very deeply."

She did not move; she did not dare.

"I knew all along that that kind of a paradise is not for a policeman, but I allowed myself to dream. I even had the thought of waiting as long as I could—as long as this arrangement continued—and then asking you if you would

199

ever consider giving up your position to become my wife. It was a dream and, like lots of dreams, it was out of reach. But for a little while it did come true. I'm very grateful for that."

"And now that there is some doubt . . ." Miriam began, but she could not finish.

"That, among other things."

She laid her hand on top of his. "Virgil, if I could know that my husband were alive and well, I couldn't and wouldn't ask for more out of life. I lived in Africa, I'm familiar with conditions there, and I'm afraid that the hope is too faint for me to take any comfort in it. I told you before that I have been reconciled to widowhood for some time. I will have to go to Switzerland—I have no choice since neither I nor my children are American citizens— and I must simply be grateful for the shelter and protection that we've been given here."

She took her hand away from his and sat gazing at the empty room, measuring her words. "If, by chance, my husband is indeed alive, then I am his, totally and completely, for as long as he wants me. That is the only way that it can be."

"I agree," Tibbs said.

"I will now tell you the truth since you have told it to me. I have done my best to keep my emotions under control, and I believe that I succeeded. But I have fallen in love with you. You knew that, of course, when I asked to share your bed.

"I will do what I should and must." She stopped again and looked at him, unable to resist doing so. "Right now there is uncertainty, and there may be for some time. When it is settled, I may be able to make some of my own decisions. It is not easy living in the eternal glare of politics. Not being able to think for myself is one of the worst restrictions."

"I understand that," Virgil told her. "You have my deepest sympathy."

"Thank you. When it is all resolved, as it will have to be someday, I want you to visit me. If possible, I want you to meet my husband so that he can thank you himself for all that you have done for me and for the children. If that isn't possible there is an alternative."

Tibbs hardly dared to breathe.

"When I know for certain that my husband is indeed dead," Miriam continued, "I will spend the rest of my life as his widow—or, if you wish it, as your wife. The choice will be yours. Please don't say anything now. I couldn't bear to hear it."

She got to her feet and walked slowly and quietly around the room, touching things with her fingers, feeling and sensing the home that she had so enjoyed and would now have to give up. She was very much locked into her own thoughts, trying once more to recover her emotional balance. She looked at the portrait over the mantel; although it belonged to Tibbs, she had come to think of it as her own. She looked into the face of the radiant young woman who had posed for it and for a moment or two, envied the freedom that was obviously hers. Then she turned back to Tibbs. "How about some lunch?" she asked.

Tibbs got up, accepting the condition that she had laid down. "Miriam, you are the world's greatest cook," he said, "but you can't make a decent milk shake. May I show you how?"

"You are the master of this house," she answered. "You show me what to do."

There's an epidemic with 27 million victims. And no visible symptoms.

It's an epidemic of people who can't read.

Believe it or not, 27 million Americans are functionally illiterate, about one adult in five.

The solution to this problem is you... when you join the fight against illiteracy. So call the Coalition for Literacy at toll-free **1-800-228-8813** and volunteer.

**Volunteer
Against Illiteracy.
The only degree you need
is a degree of caring.**

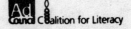

Ad Council Coalition for Literacy